four CHAMBERS

Also by Julie Wright

Death Thieves
Spell Check
Loved Like That
Tangerine Street Romance Series
Hazzardous Universe Series

four CHAMBERS

Julie WRIGHT

Heart Stone Press

Interior Design by Jules Hartman
Cover image Kaspars Grinvalds/Shutterstock
Cover design by Rachael Anderson
Published by Heart Stone Press
St. George, Utah
Printed in the United States of America
Second printing: August 2016

ISBN: 978-1-941849-06-4

To Gary,
Who toyed with the idea of going to medical school.
After all my research to write this book, I feel
you've taken the better path. I'm glad you're my
baby brother.

Other Books in the
Power of the Matchmaker Series

Broken Things to Mend by Karey White
January 2016

Not Always Happenstance by Rachael Anderson
February 2016

If We Were a Movie by Kelly Oram
March 2016

Love is Come by Heather B. Moore
April 2016

Four Chambers by Julie Wright
May 2016

O'er the River Liffey by Heidi Ashworth
June 2016

Chasing Fireflies by Taylor Dean
July 2016

Between Heaven and Earth
by Michele Paige Holmes
August 2016

How I Met Your Brother by Janette Rallison
September 2016

To Move the World by Regina Sirois
October 2016

King of the Friend Zone by Sheralyn Pratt
November 2016

The Reformer by Jaima Fixsen
December 2016

Read the matchmaker's story to find out where it all starts . . .

Mae Li has been in love with Chen Zhu for years, and he with her. But when the matchmaker arrives at the Zhu family home, she recommends another village girl for Chen.

Heartbroken, Mae Li watches as Chen does his duty by marrying another. Mae flees her village with the clothes on her back and her only possession—a pearl embedded comb, given to her as a goodbye gift from Chen Zhu.

Upon Mae's arrival in Shanghai, she quickly learns that she'll starve within days unless she sells her prized comb or joins a courtesan house. She goes to the Huangpu River and promises the River God that she'll always be selfless if he will save her from becoming a prostitute . . . Her wish is granted when Ms. Tan, the matchmaker of Shanghai, finds Mae. But Mae must completely change her future and her name if she is to become the next matchmaker.

The First Chamber

*L*ove itself is calm. It is the individuals in love who cause
the turbulence

—Chinese proverb

Chapter One

"Give me the paint," I said, hoping Janette heard the threat in my voice. She was coming seriously close to getting demoted from favorite roommate to homeless person.

"Andra, think about this for a minute." She danced out of my reach and held the paint can above her head. Pretty much anyone could do that to me. It was the curse of being five foot three. I made a jump for it, my dark ponytail swinging into my vision, causing me to miss my target. "If you spray paint the word *tool* on his truck, you'll not only get into legal trouble—arrested and fined for criminal mischief and vandalism and all that—but you'll also probably lose your scholarship, and likely your future placement at UMASS. Is that what you want?"

My hands dropped. I glared at her, glared at Greg's truck, and glared at the spray can Janette held over her head as if she believed I was still planning on coming after her and wrestling the can from her grip.

But she had me at the threat of losing my educational opportunities.

"Besides," Janette said, "You might be the youngest person in the senior class, but you're still an adult. Adults behave rationally. And you're going to be a heart surgeon someday. No one wants a heart surgeon who flies off the handle like this. It's not like you were planning on marrying this guy! So what if Greg was seen nuzzling the neck of some other girl last night?"

At the words that I'm sure Janette meant to be comforting and sensible, I lunged again for the spray paint. Janette, whose arm had lowered as she tried to talk me off the ledge of my anger, jerked her hand back and nearly fell into the street.

Everett Covington, Greg's roommate, coming back from a

morning run, arrived in time to catch her from behind. But his eyes locked on me. "Hey, Andrea without an E, what's going on?"

I just stared at him while Janette unleashed her frustration.

"You've got to talk sense into her! You've got to help me!" Janette wailed.

Everett's eyes stayed on mine, his hands still on Janette's waist. "Help you what?"

"Andra found out that Greg's been cheating on her."

Her saying it out loud to Everett felt like being stabbed in the chest all over again.

"And now she wants to spray paint the word *tool* on the side of his car. You've got to save her from herself because that's vandalism!" She continued all this with the kind of frustration that could only come from having dealt with a crazy person all Saturday night and into the morning. Neither of us slept after the phone call from a mutual friend that announced Greg to be a cheating jack-wagon.

It wasn't like I'd gone and purposely rousted my roommate from bed so she could share in my misery, but the sound of my ranting and banging cupboards had probably been hard for her to sleep through. The many threats to go over to Greg's apartment and strangle him in his sleep must have sounded real enough that Janette stayed awake with me—likely to keep me from making good on those threats. Both of us were under the pressure of exhaustion and too much emotion.

Everett listened to Janette's version of events with his face unreadable. He surveyed me from under his dark, damp hair. After a moment of some internal debate with himself, he finally plucked the can out of Janette's hand and tossed it to me. "He *is* a tool. A warning to the next girl is only fair."

I spun and started spraying.

Janette let out a roar of frustration. "Are you both stupid? This is ridiculous! You've got to stop! This is like that Carrie Underwood song where she carves her name in her boyfriend's leather seats. What kind of lunatic does something like graffiti her name into her vandalism so the police have all the evidence they need? Andra! Stop! You know I can't get into trouble for this kind of stuff. What about your scholarship? What about mine?"

I did stop then and blinked at her as if waking up from a bad dream. My situation wasn't anything like hers. If I lost my scholarship, my father would step in, find me a school who would accept me, and take over tuition payments.

I could never allow that to happen because then he would own my education. He would be able to tell me what to do and who to be. I would have to listen to him, day in and day out, tell me that my goals were too ambitious for a girl, that I wasn't made of the right kind of stuff. He would try to redirect me to other avenues that he felt more appropriate. I would hate it. It would be awful.

But it would also be survivable.

If Janette lost her scholarship, she'd have to quit school altogether, not just quit attending Boston University, because there was *no way* she could afford the tuition. Her whole life would be ruined. Unlike me, she didn't have anyone to sell her soul to, no one to pick up her pieces.

And it would be all my fault.

"Go home, Janette," I said.

"What?" She shook her head, her blonde hair frizzed from the frazzled night. Exhaustion had stolen her ability to reason. "Why?"

"If you aren't here, then you aren't involved. Go home."

I followed her gaze to where the red painted letters T O O dripped down the side of Greg's white truck like blood in a bad horror movie poster.

"Go home, Janette. I'm not taking you down with me."

"Come with me."

The tired in her voice made the tired that I'd been hiding under blind anger slam into me with full force. I lowered the paint can.

Everett, who'd been watching the whole scenario play out, took the can and finished the "L" for me.

I should've stopped him. But I hadn't even been able to muster enough self-preservation to stop *me*; I certainly didn't have the power to stop him. "Why did you do that?" I asked, staring at him like he was a puzzle on a test.

His T-shirt was stained dark at the armpits from his exercise. He crossed his arms over the Boston University logo and shrugged. "I told him you were different, that you weren't the kind of girl to be played, just because you were younger. I warned him that if he messed with you, he would deal with my wrath." He glanced back at the car and lifted his shoulder in a one-armed shrug. "My wrath looks a little pathetic now that I think about it, but . . ."

"Wrath?" I said. "Do college-aged guys feel *wrath* against cheating buddies?" I looked at Janette. "Is that even a thing?"

He shrugged again. "It's a matter of principle."

"A matter of principle leads you to painting someone's car?" Janette sounded as baffled as I felt. Had I really just done what I did? Had he really contributed to my delinquency? I hadn't even bought the cheap spray paint that would likely be more water than anything. No. I had to go and buy the good stuff so that it would stand as a testament forever to the relationship that would not last forever.

"No," he said. "A matter of principle leads me to keeping my word."

We all turned again to face the carnage of the truck. Everett tilted his head to the side as though inspecting abstract art in a museum. "So . . . do you feel better?" he asked me.

I took several deep breaths. "No," I finally answered. I threw my arms in the air. "Gah! This was really stupid. Go home, Janette. I don't want you in trouble."

"What about you?" The girl was as loyal as any best friend could ever be. If only boyfriends could be like best friends.

"I have to clean this mess up before the tool wakes up."

Everett shook his head. "You do know this isn't exactly something that can be cleaned off, right?"

I shoved at him a little. "Just go get me a bucket of soapy water and a sponge."

When he stared at me with his face clouded in doubt, I yelled, "Go. Get. A. Bucket."

With a grunt of frustration, he did as told.

Janette rubbed her hands down her face and pulled her blonde curly hair to the nape of her neck. "Sometimes, Andra, you really give me a headache."

With that declaration, she turned and left, probably to sleep for the rest of the day to make up for the night I'd stolen from her.

I collapsed down on the curb in fatigue. "Sometimes I give me a headache too."

Everett showed up moments later, sloshing sudsy water up the sides of his bucket in his obvious attempt at hurrying.

When I didn't stand to take the bucket and get to work, Everett plopped down beside me. "So Andrea without an E . . ."

"So Everest without an S . . ." I returned. The first day I'd met Everett, he'd introduced himself to me by explaining how his name required two t's. He told me to think of his name as Everest with the S replaced by a T.

I'd shared the fact that my name started as a misspelling. My name was supposed to be Andrea, but someone at the hospital wrote it wrong on my birth certificate, and my mom was too out of it with postpartum depression to care. By the time she decided she did care, my dad had decided Andra suited me better, and he wouldn't let her change it. Honestly, he probably just didn't like the name *Andrea* and purposely wrote it wrong on the certificate in the first place. He'd likely let the poor nurses take the fall so he didn't have to deal with my mother's temper. I didn't mind. I really liked my name. It was the one place of solidarity between my father and me.

Everett sighed. "Do you want to attempt to put the bucket and wash rags to use? Or do we want to let our statement stand unhindered?"

Instead of viewing our handiwork again, I focused what little remained of my drained attention on him. He finger-combed his dark hair back so that it angled across his forehead. Everett finger-combed his hair a lot—a nervous thinking habit I'd become familiar with during the many hours we'd studied together in classes we shared. I didn't really know much about Everett aside from that habit and the fact that he was really very intelligent and made a great study buddy. The angle of his hair acted as a lopsided frame for eyes that hovered between brown and gold and green. His eye color shifted as I tried to pin down which of the three colors was dominant, but it remained a mirage that could never be caught.

Everett nudged me toward where Janette had gone. "Go get some sleep. I'll keep you apprised of the events that follow. I'll even try to clean it up—though you know that's pretty much an impossibility, and we're likely going to have to pay to have his truck professionally painted to fix this. I'll do whatever you want me to."

"I'm sorry I involved you."

"I'm not. I've been wanting to do that for a long time. To have an accomplice like you just makes it perfect."

His eyes remained steady on mine. So steady, that if we made a contest of it, I knew I would be the first to blink. "Even if you have to help pay for repairs?"

"Totally worth it," he confirmed.

I closed my eyes, shutting down the visual connection between us, and leaned against Everett's shoulder, not even caring that he was a sweaty pig from his morning run. "I should've stayed the serious student," I said. "I have plans and goals. Boyfriends were never part of the plan. I don't have time for cheating tools."

He waited a moment before answering. "You know, the first date you went on with the tool was a party. And we ended up sitting on the stairs of the frat house together—just you and me, remember?"

I murmured something that I hoped counted as assent. Then I smiled and said, "Your red Solo cup was filled with peanut M&M's."

"And yours was filled with Wheat Thins."

I laughed. "That's what you get when you have two serious students wanting to be doctors at the same party."

He laughed too, but then his voice grew serious. "I asked you if you had a boyfriend. Do you remember?"

I jiggled my head against his shoulder.

"Do you remember what you answered?"

I opened my eyes as if I could somehow see the memory in front of me. "I told you I didn't because I didn't have time. Pre-med students never have time."

"True, you did mention the time thing, but you also said something that seemed kind of profound."

A garbage truck swooshed past on the road, blowing a dirty piece of notebook paper at our feet. It was crumpled and weathered from the spring rain shower yesterday, but today's sun had dried it enough to let it be blown around the street some more. The air around us smelled of recently wet stone—a smell that was familiar and comforting to me. The rainy season always brought that smell from the brownstone buildings in the Back Bay.

"I'm never profound," I said.

He ignored my self-assessment. "You said that your past boyfriends broke up with you because they felt like you weren't a dedicated enough girlfriend or whatever."

I lifted my head from off Everett's shoulder. "Is that why he cheated? Was I not dedicated enough?"

"No, Andra. He cheated because he's a tool." Everett pointed to the truck as if he needed to prove his point. "And that wasn't the profound thing you said. Stop interrupting me."

I smiled and felt a little spark of gratitude to know I still had a smile in me to give. "Sorry. Please continue telling me I'm profound."

"You said that you never felt *broken* like other girls seemed to feel at break ups. You only ever felt relieved. You said that you figured you weren't really missing anything if you couldn't even muster the ability to care, which meant you didn't really need those guys."

I remembered telling him that. I remembered the way our shoulders had been touching as we leaned back on the stairs. We were wrapped up in layers of jackets and scarves to ward off the cold humidity biting through our clothes and into our skin from the early October air. The icy chill seeped up through the cement into my jeans. I remembered really liking talking to Everett.

But Greg had found us there and laughed about Everett trying to thieve his date. Greg had taken my hand and led me back into the house.

And I hadn't looked back.

"I don't get how this is profound," I confessed. "Because I feel a little broken this time."

"Do you really? Or do you feel frustrated with school and studying and juggling the act of being the dutiful girlfriend for once in your life alongside being the serious student, just to have it backfire on you?"

I was too tired to decipher his riddles. "I don't know." The cop-out answer would have to be sufficient.

Everett put his arm around my shoulders and squeezed. "What I'm trying to say is that you don't need this guy either, Andra."

"I just don't want to be *that* girl, you know?"

"What girl?"

I grunted while searching my beaten-down mind to find an explanation. "The one who works so hard to prove she's successful at being a career-minded woman, who can handle herself in a man-dominated world, that she loses all human connections, and ends up being a frosty tyrant that other people avoid at all costs."

Everett laughed hard enough that I felt like I was encircled by a mini-earthquake. "You are definitely not going to be that girl," he affirmed.

I moved enough that Everett had to drop his arm from my shoulder. "My dad is that guy."

"Which is why you don't need to worry. You know what it's like to deal with those kinds of people, so you won't become a person like that."

I pressed the heels of my palms into my eyes, growled into my hands in frustration and finally scrambled to my feet. I eyed our artwork marking Greg's passenger door. "Do you think it'll wash off?"

"No."

Well, at least he was honest—brutal, but honest. "Do you know what sucks about being an adult and doing stupid things?" I asked.

"Hmm?" He looked up at me.

"You have to clean your own messes."

Everett laughed and got to his feet as well. We reached into the bucket for rags at the same time, our fingers touching in the sudsy water. The spark of that touch felt like someone had dropped an electronic device in with us.

I grabbed my rag and yanked my hand back out while frowning down at it. What was wrong with me?

Trying to cover up the flush I felt crawling up my neck, I turned to the truck and began to scrub at the T. I let out a little gasp of surprise. "Hey, it's coming off! I mean . . . it might take a while, but it's coming off!"

I scrubbed harder while still being careful to not scrub so hard, I actually drilled down into the real paint. Everett began working on the L so we weren't bumping elbows into each other. After many long minutes, the two O's looked like eyes with little shadow ear lines next to them. I almost wanted to paint matching pupils into those eyes.

Everett dropped his rag with a wet squelch and pulled his phone from his pocket. "There has got to be a YouTube video for how to get spray paint off a car." He stared at his screen, his finger swiping over it now and again until he broke into a grin. "Aha! Fingernail polish remover."

He tossed a wink to me and shook his head. "Seriously, what did people do before YouTube tutorials?"

"My father says the internet fails to separate the wheat from the chaff because no one has to figure stuff out for themselves anymore."

"Yeah, well, your father's wrong. It's not about knowing everything. It's about knowing where to look when you need answers."

I appreciated that he said my father was wrong. Not many people dared. "Well, it's no surprise. My father is wrong about everything."

"Not everything. He brought you into existence."

I shot Everett what I hoped was a withering look. "I know you're trying to make me feel better, but that was over the top."

Everett shrugged. "Maybe a little. I'll just go get the nail polish remover."

I wiped my hair from my eyes, accidentally dripping sudsy water over the bridge of my nose and having to wipe that away too. "Why do you have nail polish remover?"

Everett halted, clearly not anticipating being asked such a question. "It's my prerogative to not disclose that information. I'll be back in a minute." He started up the stone steps of the house he and Greg shared.

"Hey Everest?"

He turned and tilted his head to the side in his familiar gesture of questioning.

"Thanks . . . you know . . . for being my friend through all of this."

He paused for what seemed a long time before coming to some decision. "You know all those many months ago when we were sitting on the stairs to that party on your first date with Greg?"

"Yeah?"

"I was planning on asking you out."

I blinked, confused by this news, unsure what to do with it. But before I could reply, he'd already turned and disappeared behind the door.

I leaned down and picked up the spray paint can from off the curb and stared down at what I held. In one hand was the can of red spray paint, still cold inside from expelling its energy. In the other was the sudsy rag that had gone a little pink with the scrubbing.

In my hands was both the mess and the solution.

I had become Greg's girlfriend.

Everett had planned to ask me out.

Some part of me had known that at the party. Some part of me had been glad to make a Solo cup toast with Wheat Thins and peanut M&M's.

I was still blinking in confusion when the police car turned the corner of Greg's street with its siren on and lights flashing, jolting to a halt right in front of Greg's truck.

I tightened my grip on the paint can and the wash rag, squared my shoulders, and faced what was coming.

Chapter Two

The neighbors had called the cops on us, and I was intensely glad I'd sent Janette home.

When Everett came out with the bottle of nail polish remover to find me being apprehended by the lady cop, he halted so hard, he spilled the already uncapped bottle down the front of him. The wet swath darkened his jeans, and I worried it would discolor the dark blue denim. I wanted to tell him to go inside and change into something else so he could hurry and rinse his pants, but I didn't want to draw attention to him, didn't want anyone to see that the only person I felt any degree of friendliness toward in my current circumstances was Everett.

If the police thought Everett was my friend, they would think he'd been an accomplice—which he *was*, but no one else needed to know that information.

Unfortunately, the lady cop with the severe bun that likely gave her a headache noticed him and called him down the stairs to join us.

"What do you have to do with this?" she asked before his foot made it to the bottom step.

His glance slid toward and away from me as he opened his mouth to say something that was surely incriminating.

"He caught me while I was painting!" I yelled it as if by shouting my confession, I would be able to get it out faster than he could get out his.

"Yes," I said and nodded as if agreeing with myself. "Yes, he caught me and then got me a bucket and water so I could clean it up. That's also why he has nail polish remover. He was pretty unhappy with me for ruining his friend's truck, and he talked some sense into me and convinced me that I needed to take responsibility for my actions. And then he decided to help me clean it up because he's a genuinely nice person." I nodded some more and forced myself to look penitent.

With the nail polish remover in his hands and the fact that I did indeed have a wash bucket with water and soap and had been scrubbing at the truck, the lady cop had no reason to suspect my story and she moved back to where the guy cop stood.

"What are you doing?" Everett whispered.

"There's no reason for both of us to be in trouble."

"I can take the heat for my own actions."

"Yes, but now if you tell the truth, you'll make me look like a liar, and I'll get into even more trouble. So keep your do-gooder attitude out of this, okay?"

He closed his mouth with a click of his teeth. The muscles in his jaw tightened with his irritation at me for yanking him out of the equation. Idiot Everest. It was like he *wanted* to get kicked out of school.

A frothing, sleep-addled Greg hurled himself out his front door. His eyes were wild. "My truck!" He brayed the words, his mouth hanging open, his wild eyes wide in disbelief. "Andra? What's going on?"

I silently watched him without answering. Watched the way he flailed his arms and demanded answers. Watched the way he crooned and cried over a piece of metal used for transportation. And watched how he had immediately assumed I did the horrible defacing deed.

I mean, I *had* done it. But if he'd had any loyalty toward me at all, shouldn't he have assumed I'd come upon the crime scene and caught a delinquent perpetrator. Didn't the fact that, without hesitation, he painted me as the delinquent perpetrator mean something?

Only two reasons existed for him to think I was guilty of acting the part of a jilted lover. One, he was guilty of doing the jilting. And two, he didn't really care about me to begin with.

"My truck! Andra! How could you? Why does it say OO? What does that even mean? You know what this truck means to me! You know how much I love this truck!" He wailed these words like a paid mourner.

He didn't even stop when Everett said, "Dude, it's a truck. Kind of not important in the long term, you know. Don't you think you and Andra should have a different kind of conversation? You know . . . the kind where you explain to her what happened with Allyson last night?"

"Allyson?" He blinked in confusion as to why Everett would bring up the other woman in my presence. "I don't know what that . . ."

Everett spoke slowly, as if talking to a child. I would've laughed except the lady cop took me by the arm and sat me down on the curb as if I was going to flee the crime scene and sitting me down would make such an action impossible, or at least more difficult.

I turned to face Everett and Greg so I could observe the conversation.

"Allyson, you know, from last night?" Everett continued. "You have to understand that Andra had a reason to act as she did. You have to know she would not have damaged your property without sufficient evidence to make her angry. Aren't you going to ask her why she felt angry? Aren't you the least bit curious as to why she's angry?"

The guy cop showed up. "This is your vehicle?" he said to Greg which set Greg back to wailing over the piteous condition of his ride.

There were questions, paperwork filled out, more questions.

Sitting on a curb with the policewoman and policeman moving around me and doing their jobs while neighbors and onlookers came to gawk at the free ticket to a real-life drama wasn't really as bad as I'd imagined it might be.

A little embarrassing, sure.

A little flustering, absolutely.

But Everett had been right.

I wasn't broken.

As Greg grabbed handfuls of his golden, wavy hair—the same hair the little tramp had been running her fingers through last night—and asked me over and over again why I would do such a hateful thing, I considered all the emotions inside me.

And found myself not really feeling much of anything.

Did that make me a sociopath?

Did that make me incapable of real human connection?

Was I already a frosty tyrant?

I peeked a glance at Everett as he hovered around the edges of the circus I'd created and gnawed on his already-gnawed fingernails—another of his nervous study habits. He'd already been wrung out entirely, shaken down by both the police and by Greg, who wanted to know what his involvement in the vandalism had been. I maintained loudly, and in a tone that commanded authority, that Everett had come upon me while I was in the act and then rushed in to get something to clean it up so it wouldn't dry and become permanent.

The cops believed me.

Everett scowled at me.

Greg ranted at me.

At the end of the day, I was cited for a misdemeanor of vandalism, but I wasn't arrested, and they didn't slap the felony charge that they could have on me. The fact that I had the washcloth in my hands was evidence to my intent to make retribution. The fact that Everett had the nail polish remover, which worked like the sorcery of a candy house on little German children, gave evidence to the fact that he was innocent in everything. The fact that we were able to clean up the mess meant a lesser charge against me.

A citation.

I didn't think a citation sounded so bad. Not anything worse than a traffic violation. Surely that would not jeopardize my standing in school.

When the circus had played out all of its various acts, the police issued a no trespass on me. This meant I was not allowed to enter the vicinity of Greg's personal property ever again, or at least not until further notice.

Then they sent me home.

And for the first time since knowing Everett, I looked back as I was leaving him.

Looked back and wondered.

I should've never gone into the house with Greg all those months ago, I thought. I should've stayed and seen what might have happened with someone different.

But that time to choose was gone.

Sorry, Everett, I thought. And, as if he heard my thoughts, his mouth turned down into something so sad, it almost made me want to cry.

So. I wasn't totally frosty.

Not yet.

Chapter Three

Four days after Bad-Judgment Day, I absently answered a call from an unknown number. My stomach sank into my toes as the voice on the other end invited me to visit the office of the dean over the school of medicine at Boston University. By *invite*, the dean's secretary meant that if I failed to show up, I might as well never show up to another class again.

Of course I went and went early to prove myself to be a responsible person who could keep things like appointments.

Dean Jasmine Connery, known by the students as Jazzy Dean, stared me down from over her laptop when I entered her office. She closed the lid with a click and folded her hands neatly on top. The volumes lining the shelves behind her sagged on the shelves as if they'd been there since the Revolutionary War.

"Well," she began.

Well indeed.

She used words like disappointed, baffled, and saddened by my destructive behavior toward another student. How could I, a model exemplary student with so much potential, be capable of such reprehensible criminal mischief?

I embarrassed the school.

I threatened my scholarship.

I made her look bad through my outrageous and inexcusable behavior.

She had seen so much potential in me since I graduated high school with an associate degree that boasted top grades and since I had maintained that high academic standard while completing my bachelor's.

I had utterly let her, and the school, down.

Egregious. Contemptible. Shameful. Shocking. Despicable.

I left her office scarred with a knowledge that all those adjectives were deserved. I tucked my hands into the sleeves of my sweater, feeling cold in spite of the warm day and bent my head to walk to my apartment, crawl into my bed, and die a little.

"I came as soon as I found out."

The words startled me out of my self-loathing. "Everett?" He leaned against a tree, as if he'd been waiting for me. "What are you doing here?"

He shoved off the tree and hurried to join me on the sidewalk. "Greg was talking to one of his friends about how he made sure Jazzy Dean found out about the incident with his truck. She never would have known if he hadn't called since the incident happened off-campus and you were only slapped on the wrist. I can't begin to express how much I hate that guy right now. So what happened? Is everything okay? Do you need me to go and confess to my part in it? Because I will. Whatever you need, I'll do."

It warmed me a little to know that someone cared, someone had my back in this crazy mess. Even Greg's extra dig at me failed to hurt as much as it might have if Everett hadn't been there. "Don't worry about it. She just wanted to yell at me. I'm not kicked out or anything."

"What about your scholarship? Is that okay?"

That was the kicker. "I don't know," I said. We began walking under the newly budding trees that smelled like honey and New England springtime.

"What does that mean?"

"My scholarship isn't only academic, it's also a community-based scholarship, which means my actions in the community affect my eligibility to keep the scholarship." I pulled a few pink buds off a low hanging limb and shredded them between my fingers.

"And what does that mean?" He said the words slowly, deliberately, as if he feared the answer.

"It means she will be talking to her review board, and they will be making a decision based on all the information."

Review boards seldom chose mercy when justice made such a better example to everyone else.

"I'm so sorry, Andra."

Our walking became aimless, the meandering of my lost spirit taking form in the actual path we trod.

"It's my own fault. I bought the paint and didn't stop to think about the long term consequences."

We were turned toward the BU beach and walked until I felt

too tired under the strain of what might happen with the review board. I sat on the grass and stared out over Storrow Drive toward the river.

"But how could you have guessed he'd call the dean?" Everett asked, settling beside me.

"I should have known, though. I'm smart, right? Isn't that what all of this is about?" I waved my hand to the campus around us. "Smart girls don't go revenge-of-the-jilted-girlfriend on idiot boyfriends. Smart girls finish their degrees and become successful pediatric heart surgeons while the idiot is still trying to figure out what the acronym MCAT stands for."

I growled and fell back to the grass so I could stare at the blue sky and feel stupid for the bad decision to date Greg.

As though he'd become my shadow, Everett lay on the grass beside me and turned his body toward mine with his head propped on his arm. "You're exaggerating. He knows what MCAT stands for."

"He does now. But only because I told him. Before we started dating, he thought it stood for *masters* or *major*. He seriously couldn't even guess the medical part."

"Huh. Well now I'm just embarrassed for him. So . . . smart girl. I know you're already making plans for either decision the board comes back with; care to share?"

I rolled over to face him and sucked in a deep breath to find him so close to me. But I didn't scoot away. I tucked my arm under my head and shrugged. "There aren't good plans. But there are plans."

He didn't prod me for more, but simply waited. Some guys tossed a football just down from us, their yells and laughter bouncing off and around the buildings and back in our direction.

"My dad," I explained. "He's the backup plan. Which means I will have to listen to all the reasons why a heart surgeon is far too ambitious for me and how I should reconsider my future."

"Too ambitious? For you? How can anyone say that? You're three years younger and at the top of the class."

He was close enough that I could smell his mint toothpaste as he spoke. He must have dressed and come right over when he found out what Greg had done. It made me glad I had not only brushed my teeth, but also flossed and swished mouthwash. "Top of the class doesn't mean much. It's about the position in the family. I am one of two children. And I'm the youngest. And I'm the girl. My parents are what you would call extremely traditional, and we come from old money. My mom wanted a debutante. My dad wanted a little boy who he could raise to be a brilliant doctor just like him. They wanted me to learn how to say pretty things at parties with lots of other influential debutantes. They wanted my brother to get all the degrees and achievements. And they are incredibly disappointed in the children they ended up with."

He didn't argue with me. He didn't try to say I was wrong and that surely my parents loved me just as I was. He didn't try to make my situation bright and shiny. He simply let it be.

I never appreciated anything more.

He also didn't give me the whole *oh, poor you, born with a silver spoon in your mouth and not liking the palace you were raised in* that some people gave me. Most people who knew who my parents were assumed I lived on the parental dole.

What they didn't know was that I had taken care of my own finances since I turned sixteen and was legally allowed to get a job, just to give myself the freedom of making my own choices.

And it was worth it.

Except if the board yanked the scholarship out from under my feet, I would be forced to either give up my educational dreams altogether, or swallow that bitter glass of pride and accept my parents' help.

"And look at you now," Everett said, half of his smile disappearing behind his elbow.

He couldn't know how those words cut me at that moment where looking at myself made me feel incredibly sick. I took the words for how he'd intended them and not how they made me feel. "And look at my brother, too. He's a culinary chef with his own YouTube channel that has more followers than Adele. He's doing great, but he's not doing what my dad wants."

"So wouldn't your dad want to make sure you at least followed the doctor dream? At least then one of his kids would be redeemable in his eyes, although I can't see why anyone would turn down having a chef in the family. Think of those Christmas dinners . . ."

I picked at the blades of grass under my hand. "That's just it. He doesn't consider a girl doing those things as redeemable. He thinks I'm taking part in an unnatural rebellion."

Everett let out a laugh that didn't sound as if he found anything actually funny. "You should have been born into my family. My mom is the greatest women's rights activist on the planet."

"Lucky."

"Not for me lucky, but my sisters . . . yeah, lucky them."

The football game that had been just down from us was now suddenly in the middle of us as a football landed right between Everett and me.

We both jumped and sat up. A guy in basketball shorts and a tank top jogged over, "Hey sorry about that, man."

"No problem." Everett threw the ball back and returned his attention to me. "Anyway, so your backup plan is your dad. It sucks, but at least you have options."

"Kind of. He thinks I'm too young to be on my own. He'll want me to go to school closer to home."

"Connecticut?"

"Good memory. Yeah. My family's from Connecticut. If he's buying, I'll have to change schools." I pulled my knees to my chest and wrapped my arms around them.

"But you're almost done here."

I shrugged. No one could ever accuse my father of being rational. But I didn't say that out loud. What did it matter? I only sighed.

"Maybe the board will decide to give you a pass on this one incident. You've never been in trouble before. Maybe you'll get a warning. I mean, c'mon, his truck is fine. No real damage done."

"Maybe." I didn't believe that would be the outcome. School boards couldn't afford to look the other way in cases of criminal activity. It opened too many floodgates for other infractions to be overlooked and their reputation would be blackened. I knew what they would decide. And I couldn't even really blame them.

Everett stood and swept the grass clippings off his jeans. "C'mon." He held out his hand.

I stared at it. "C'mon what?"

"We are going to go have some fun. We've both worked hard all semester and deserve a break."

I still didn't take his hand. "I don't need a break. I need to get to work, to prove I'm worthy to keep my scholarship."

He jiggled his hand in front of my face. "It isn't like the board has hired a private investigator to see if you've jumped right back into studies after nearly getting cuffed and hauled to jail. They only see your grades. And since you and I have almost all the same classes, I know you have only one class today, and it's totally missable because all we're doing is handing in reports and discussing the reading. And if I know anything about you at all, you've already uploaded your report, and it's better than everyone else's, and you've already got 100 points in extra credit and you've never missed a day in your life, even though the professor gives us two 'escape days.'"

He was right. I had never missed a day of class. This semester was nearly over. My assignments were all done.

I took his hand and did something I'd never done in my life.

I acted irresponsibly.

Well, I acted irresponsibly for the second time in my life, since painting *tool* on Greg's truck was totally irresponsible.

But this was different, because no anger preceded this moment, no emotional trauma compelled me forward through an act that I knew was out of my character. This was different because it promised something new, something fun, something unknown.

Anything new had to be good.

As I let Everett lead me away, I gave the slightest tug on my hand so he knew he could let go if he wanted to.

But he didn't let go.

His fingers tightened over mine.

And I laughed. For the first time in a long, long time.

Chapter Four

He walked me to the DeWolfe boathouse.

"Everett . . ." I started, pulling back a little. I didn't have a row class, though I'd been tempted to take the class just for the excuse to start my day on the Charles River, but my classes never lined up well enough to allow me the opportunity.

"What, you scared of the water?" Everett asked.

"No, I just don't have a class here. I don't think we're supposed to be in here if we don't have a class."

"We're okay, Andrea without an E. Trust me. I'm not going to get you in trouble with campus police when you're already stressing about losing your scholarship. I promise you won't get kicked out of school on top of everything else. He tightened his hand on mine and tugged me closer to him until our noses were only inches apart, until I could see his eyes shifting colors from green to brown to gold and back again.

I had the insane urge to close the distance between us. Startled at the unbidden thought, I backed up a little and said, "Course I trust you." I cleared my throat. What kind of girl wants to lip-lock with her ex's roommate only two days after the break up?

Andra Stone was not that girl. And she never would be that girl.

I gave my head a sharp nod as if I'd made a pact with myself. Good. I hadn't *totally* forgotten myself.

Everett led me inside the door to the boathouse.

The room we entered was spacious with several staircases, one leading down directly in front of us, and two on either side of us, leading up. A bank of exercise machines to the left were in use by a couple of students. I nodded and tried to smile as though I wasn't the interloper that I actually was. The smell of wet and wood and New England soaked the air. Everett waved at the guy and girl on the workout machines and headed down the stairs as if he owned the place.   "Hey!" he called out once we were in the basement. "Hey, Renee! Are you down here?" He led us through the maze of stacked row boats and oars, searching out the person named Renee.

A female voice from around the stacks of rowboat shells called back. "Ev! Is that you?"

"Yeah, it's me."

A girl giggle filled the entire basement in a way that reminded me of champagne bubbles.

"I knew you'd come! I've been waiting for you to take me up on my offer to borrow the boats during off time so that we—"

She rounded the corner and stopped short when she saw me. "Oh. You're with someone." She fixed him with a look that should have frozen the water under the boathouse all the way to the silt and said in tones so icy, I actually shivered. "So who's this?"

Either Everett was totally oblivious to the fact that this girl really liked him and him bringing me in here made her furious, or he was a callous creep who didn't care about the feelings of others.

Everything I knew about Everett told me it was the first option. He was completely unaware that she felt any attraction to him.

Which was something new.

Greg had always been hyper-aware of how other girls viewed him. A flirty waitress in a restaurant made him smile wider. A pretty jogger smiling at him on the trail along the river made him square his shoulders and put a strut to his jogger gait. One of his roommates' girlfriends batted eyelashes his direction, and he was right there to tell her jokes and keep her entertained until his roommate came down to claim the girl—the girl who always took a last lingering look at Greg before she left with the guy she'd intended to be with.

It had never really bothered me because out of all those girls who competed for his attention, I was the one he chose to be with.

It made me feel bad to see this girl looking at me like I was encroaching on her territory. It was outright agony to watch her eyes drop from Everett's face to our hands linked together between us. I forced Everett to let go of my hand as I reached out to take hers and introduce myself. "I'm Andra Stone. We're just friends."

"Oh," she said. Her face brightened.

"Right," he said. His face didn't brighten.

"What are you guys doing today?" she asked.

Everett looked down at my hand hanging loosely at my side until I folded my arms across my chest, and he turned his attention back to Renee. "Andra, my *friend*, has always wanted to take a row class but she refuses to carve time into her schedule for herself, so I wanted to give her a glimpse into how great rowing is, so that she actually makes time for the class next term."

"Freshman?" Renee asked, still a little wary of my position in Everett's life.

"Senior." I corrected her.

"Wow. You look really young." She shot Everett a look that could be interpreted as, *"She's a kid. Stay away from jail bait."*

Technically, I was *too* young to be a senior. Getting two years of college out of the way when I was in high school sped things along nicely. But I wasn't about to tell her I had just barely celebrated my twentieth birthday, not when every glance cast in my direction felt like a dissection.

She sighed as if in deep regret. "You know I can't let you take a shell out on your own—even for a prospective rowing student."

Which was directly in conflict with what she'd been saying she could do before she saw me.

Everett didn't seem bothered by her lack of enthusiasm. "I'll check it out, nice and legal. I want a two man sculling boat." He handed her his student ID.

She sucked in her cheeks as though biting into them hard and turned and said, "Fine. Two man sculling." She walked around to one of the other rooms and pointed at one of the boats.

"We're going to get into that?" I felt apprehension once faced with the contraption they called a boat. It wasn't much wider than a broomstick handle.

Everett took the boat down. "Yeah. It'll be fun."

"It's not very wide though, is it?"

Renee smirked at my apparent ignorance.

Everett didn't smirk. "You've seen the row teams out on the water, haven't you?"

Of course I had seen them, every morning on my way to classes, but the boats looked wider from a distance.

He carried the boat through the large open bay doors that led to the water. Not wanting to stand in the boathouse with Renee smirking at me, I hurried after him. He seemed perfectly at ease as he settled the boat into the water and placed the oars in their brackets. He took off his shoes and placed them at the front of the boat. "You'll want to take off your shoes, as well," he said.

I sat down and did as directed. "Are we going to end up in the water?" I asked

"Not unless you rock us over," he answered.

I thought I heard a laugh from inside the boathouse bay doors and wondered if Renee had called the people from upstairs to come watch a newb enter the waters. They were probably taking bets on how long it would be before I tipped us.

"How do you know how to do this?" I asked.

Everett tightened in the last oar and smiled at me. "I was on the novice row team my freshman and sophomore years. I make a point of taking one class for fun every semester."

"Oh. Right. Makes sense." Taking a class for pleasure to help offset the stress did make sense. I just didn't have the time for that kind of sense.

"Okay," Everett said, holding one set of oars, but looking at me. "I want you to go in first so I can help you and keep you steady. It's easy."

"Easy huh?"

Another laugh from within the boathouse made my ears burn with anger. The competitive side of me kicked in. Renee had no idea who she was dealing with. I wasn't going to let some Everett-girlfriend-wannabe make me feel stupid. "Okay," I said, "what do I do?"

He explained about weight and keeping it centered in the right place and holding the oars so the one stays on the stage and the other stays flat on the water to provide extra balance. After a few false starts where I realized the seat was on rails that made it move around, which complicated everything for me, I finally made it onto a seat, and no one went swimming in the effort.

Take that Everett-girlfriend-wannabe.

Everett gave me a few instructions regarding the oars and how to keep them in my hands at all times in order to keep the boat balanced and how not to push down on them too far or I would end up soaked.

Everett settled onto the seat behind me, and we were ready to go.

"Okay. We need to push off away from the stage," he said.

When I tried to push off and we didn't really go anywhere, Everett's laugh joined Renee's.

"No, sorry. My fault for not explaining. Boats aren't made to go sideways. So we angle in at the stern and push back." As he said the words, he shoved against the deck and propelled us backwards.

It wasn't like we were going very fast, but we *were* going backwards, and I felt incredibly unsteady. I inhaled a sharp breath that I could not seem to make myself exhale.

Everett laughed again. "It's okay to breathe, Andrea without an E."

"If you keep laughing at me, you'll be the one not breathing, Everest without an S."

He laughed again.

My teeth chattered entirely from fear. Everett dipped in his oars and we were off.

I did exactly as he told me, relying on my own sense of balance to keep us upright in spite of the fact that we were skimming the water on a broom stick. I didn't add much in the way of rowing since the few times I tried to be helpful in that area nearly dropped us into the river. But after a while, the speed over the water and the wind blowing my hair back off my neck felt so freeing that I even forgot to be worried about losing my scholarship.

He slowed as we neared the bridge. As we passed under the words *Make History* graffitied on the side of the train bridge that I had seen every time I walked this way down the river, I wished I dared turn around to peek at Everett, but didn't dare for fear I'd offset the boat.

Everett was a *make history* kind of guy.

"Novice, huh?" I asked.

"I'm a skilled novice," he said.

He slid us easily under the shade of the bridge and back out into the sun. And he slowed even more until we drifted along under the second bridge, which was concrete instead of metal. "I bet the acoustics in here are good," I said.

"Sing me something, and I'll keep us here a minute so we can find out." He worked the oars in a way that made us stand still in the water.

"I don't really sing." I was glad he couldn't see my face and the blush that warmed it.

"You don't really tell the truth either because I've heard you sing, and you're pretty good."

"When have you heard?"

"Whenever you're thinking through a problem, you hum to yourself."

I gripped my oars tighter, only not because I was afraid of falling into the water. I was afraid of falling into something else. Something that seemed wrong to want in light of everything that had happened. He really had been paying attention during the time I spent with Greg. "It's strange to talk with you when you're behind me," I said, trying to ease the conversation away to something that didn't make me feel so exposed.

"That's why it should be easier for you to sing. You don't even have to look at me."

I hummed a few bars from the song "For Good" from *Wicked*.

"Oh, I like that one. Sing that."

"I just did," I insisted as I twisted slightly to look at him. The boat tilted, and I froze and slowly faced forward again.

"No, you introduced it. I want to hear you sing."

"And if I refuse?"

"How stubborn are you?" he asked. "Because *I* am pretty stubborn. I can keep us here in the water all day. You'll have to either swim or sing to see shore again."

"You're holding me hostage?"

He didn't answer.

"I'm stubborn, too," I finally said.

But, as it turned out, Everett was more stubborn.

The water snaked around us as we hovered in the same place for a long, long, long time.

"I've heard it said . . ." I began singing.

The smug rolled off him and filled the space between the water and the bridge.

He joined me in the second verse, and I learned something new about Everett.

He had a beautiful voice, the kind that made me stop singing a moment just so I could listen to him.

When the song ended, neither of us spoke, and then we were moving again, slicing through the water in Everett's steady rhythm that felt like a song of its own.

When we returned to the *stage*, as Everett called it, Renee showed no signs of the jealousy that she'd displayed earlier. She must have had time to deal with it while we were gone. But she did seem a bit disappointed that not only hadn't we flipped while out on the open water, I managed to not flip us while getting out either.

As soon as the sculling boat was dried and put back in its place in the boathouse and Everett had retrieved his student ID, he took my hand again as though it was the most natural thing in the world.

Renee's eyes narrowed at the gesture, but this time, I didn't let go of his hand to try to please her. My competitive streak really wasn't the best part of my personality.

From the boathouse, Everett took me to the rock climbing wall at the FitRec, and he also took me to the bouldering structure where we tried out the crash pads and laughed more than I think I'd laughed in my whole life.

"I had no idea any of this was even on campus," I admitted as we walked away.

"That's because all you do is study."

"Hey, I don't always study. I go out sometimes. How else do you think I had a boyfriend?"

The words were out before I knew I was saying them, but they made me stop and frown and feel awkward. "Of course that boyfriend cheated, so what does that say about me? Maybe I do study too much."

Everett laced his fingers in mine and leaned down so he could force me to look him in the eye. "What you had was a guy who never showed you anything new and never added adventure to your life, who never worried about you needing a break or a diversion. He failed you because he let status quo stay . . . quo. What it says about you is that you are better off. That's all. Just that. What it says about him is a lot more and a lot worse."

"Why, Everest?"

Everett tilted his head in question to my question.

"Why are you doing all this for me?"

"I told you. When we met, all three of us, you, Greg, me, in our organic chemistry class, I was planning on asking you out. I was in the process of doing the actual asking when Greg interrupted and beat me to the invite. I've been waiting a while to spend time with you."

I'm not sure what I said after that. Did I say anything? Did I squeak out a word or a syllable? He didn't seem to want or expect a response. With our fingers laced together, we walked through the campus to the street and over to the Bees Knees for some lunch at their café.

And I hadn't even mentioned to Everett that the Bees Knees was my favorite.

Part of me wondered if he knew because Greg had said something or if he'd overheard me say something in the past, or if maybe this was just something we had in common.

And part of me wondered why I had to overthink everything.

It was just really hard not to overthink things when everything felt so fast. How I'd gone from getting into trouble with Jazzy Dean and having the worst day in human history to holding hands with a nice guy and having fun, *real life fun*, simply seemed . . . way too fast.

The day was kind of perfect, in spite of its blemished beginnings. Everett and I never ran out of things to talk about, and when he walked me home that evening, I realized I hadn't thought about needing to do my homework once. I hadn't worried about my dad taking over my education. I hadn't felt panicked or stricken over the fact that I played hooky from class.

"So, you going to be okay?" he asked.

"I think so. No matter what happens, it isn't the end of the world. Right?"

"You seem a little more relaxed than you did this morning." He leaned against the wrought iron railing and surveyed me.

"Honestly, I feel like I just finished a day session at my mother's spa sanctuary." I exhaled a deep breath. Spa days were the one thing I actually missed from home.

"Well . . . I'm glad I could be here with you to enjoy a good day."

I laughed. "Let's be honest. In spite of the whole police part, painting Greg's car with you was a pretty good day, too."

He smiled a smile that had to have cost his parents a fortune to achieve. I'd never really thought about his smile before, but now that I was looking, he had a pleasant face.

I smiled too, knowing mine was equal to his. My parents had spent a fortune on my mouth, as well.

My gaze slid up to his eyes to find he was looking at my mouth as much as I had been looking at his.

Everett pushed lightly off the railing and leaned in close enough for me to really smell him.

He smelled like cinnamon and cloves. I couldn't help it; I breathed deeper, filling my senses with the scent that was him.

"What are you doing?' he asked. I could hear the grin in his words.

"You smell like something caught between a Mediterranean dish my mom likes to cook and Christmas Eve."

He tucked his head closer to mine so that our cheeks touched and whispered, "And you smell like a lemonade stand."

My eyes fluttered closed as his breath, warm and promising, breezed against my ear.

I forced myself to stand back a little so as not to lose myself in a moment I might have been overthinking. "So why do you smell like Christmas?"

"My aftershave. It's the only scent that doesn't smell like teenage-boy-trying-too-hard. Why do you smell like the lemonade stand from my Boy Scout fundraiser?"

"You were a Boy Scout?"

"I did a ten minute tour of the Scouting program, yes."

"Huh. One more thing I did not know about you. The lemon you smell is because my mom's a diehard vegan who believes in essential oils. She has some natural, holistic, eco-friendly body lotion she buys that she adds essential oils to. She always sends me the lemon scented ones because I don't much like the others."

"Maybe I was wrong about you." His eyes dropped to my

lips, and the moment slowed slightly to something cozy again—
something safe.

"Wrong?"

Every word brought him closer. "I thought you would never be interested in me." At the word *me*, his bottom lip brushed against mine so softly, I might have just imagined it.

"Then yes, you were wrong," I whispered.

Chapter Five

When the phone rang early Friday afternoon, I had no idea who the number belonged to. I ignored the ring.

It rang again.

I turned the volume off. Homework at the kitchen table was sacred time for Janette and me. Anyone who knew me well, knew not to call during study hours. And people who didn't know me well didn't make the short list of obligatory phone answering.

"Aren't you going to get that?" Janette asked.

"Nope."

"Who is it?"

"I don't know. That's why I'm not going to get it." I pulled two Wheat Thins from the near-empty box and stuffed them into my mouth when the phone screen lit up to indicate the caller was making a third attempt.

"What if it's important?"

"Then they'll leave a voicemail, like the rest of civilized society." I returned to the twelfth edition of advanced microbiology, which likely wasn't any different from the eleventh edition, and ate a few more Wheat Thins. Studying had been hard enough since kissing Everett. That sizzling moment was all I could think about. The scene replayed over and over and over in my head, enough that I worried Janette would catch the stupid grin on my face and ask me to explain why it existed. I didn't feel ready to explain the situation with Everett.

"Most people in society aren't civilized," Janette said.

"Then I'm doing myself a favor by not forcing myself to talk to them." I turned the page.

She tapped on her sixth edition nutritionist's book and narrowed her eyes at the Wheat Thins box. "Those aren't actually healthy."

"It says 'low sodium choice' on the box." I didn't look up from my book. "Besides I like it, and you've ruined enough foods for me by lecturing on their contents. You leave this one alone."

"I didn't say it was *unhealthy*. I just said—"

My phone lit up again.

Janette sighed at the device as if it was guilty of something terribly naughty. "Do you want me to answer it?"

I smiled. "Nope." Answering the phone was out of the question. After my brush with the law, I answered one call with a phone number I didn't recognize. That had been the phone call inviting me to meet with Jazzy Dean over my delinquent behavior. I needed time to prepare myself for another such call.

My phone went blessedly blank and nothing alerted me to any voicemails, meaning I was safe from dean tyranny for a little while longer.

A short while later, our doorbell buzzed. Janette scraped her chair back on the hardwood floor that had been abused by that girl since we moved in, and answered the door. We had other roommates, but they used the apartment as more of a storage space for their stuff. They were never home, which was fine because Janette hadn't liked either one of them.

"Andra!" she called from the entryway. "This one's definitely for you."

My stomach soured. Was it campus police? Real police? Greg's dad, who had given him the truck in the first place? Reluctantly, I stood and went to face the music, whatever it might be.

It turned out the music was a plastic bucket filled with cans of red spray paint, and a note.

Roses are red
Spray paint is too
If we do time
I hope it's together
(If you don't like the poem, just remember I'm premed, not liberal arts.)

Come out with me tonight. I was even good and waited until your classes and study hours were over.

P.S. put my number in your phone and actually answer!

"I don't know," I said in response to Janette's look of *explain yourself now*. "I really don't know except he helped me through a really rough past few days, and I don't know how to explain how I feel when I'm with him except to say that when I'm not with him, I want to be, you know?"

"You sure you're not rebounding?"

How could anyone be sure of such a thing? Except I didn't feel like I was rebounding; it felt like *bounding*—for the first time.

I held my bucket of paint can flowers, picked at the top of one of the lids and shrugged.

She shook her head and went back inside. "You gotta give the guy credit," she called over her shoulder. "The paint cans are cute."

They were more than cute. They were perfect. And the poem was funny. And the guy kissed me in a way that made me feel cherished. "I have my grams's seventy-second birthday party tonight." I stared mournfully at the spray paint cans and clutched them a little tighter to me.

"You can always ask him to go with you. It would make your mom happy to see you have a date. "She might think you've finally decided to do your obligation as a woman by marrying a successful doctor and give up the upstart, pretentious notion of actually being one." She smirked at me and rolled her eyes.

I frowned hard enough to give me a headache. "There's a reason *not* to take him."

"You could always take the paint cans, too. If your mom gets out of hand, you and Everett already know how to use them and clearly have no scruples about the whole thing."

I laughed. "I think you're on to something."

"At least we now know who's been calling." Janette flopped down on her chair and fixed her eyes back on the pages of her book.

I sat in my chair across from her. "If I take him, would I be doing something stupid?"

She eyed me over the top of her book before putting it back down. "No. I think you are making the first smart relationship choice you've ever made. Greg was an emotional thug. He pick-pocketed your feelings and didn't even leave you fare for the T. Everett's a nice guy. He has always taken an interest in you. The question is, what are you looking for?"

"What do you mean?"

"You've got just under a semester for your undergraduate, four years of med school, another five of residency, and another two of specialized residency. Twelve years is a long time."

Twelve years was a long time. It felt like a lifetime away when I would belong to myself again. But if I never dated or had human relationships, I would turn into that frosty tyrant I worried lurked underneath my skin. "Why didn't you mention any of this when I was dating Greg?"

"Greg is a transitory boyfriend. The kind whose fun to kiss and nice to look at, but who is ultimately a go-nowhere road. Everett is a guy with possibilities. So, while I like him and think he's good for you, the question you have to ask yourself is a simple one: are you a surgeon, or not?"

"I'm a surgeon." The words came out in a defensive bite.

"Of course you are. I just know you have a mom who would be delighted to see you settled down with a doctor and doing your job of making his friends and colleagues martinis at parties you're hosting at your house. The one she would buy you so you didn't have to do anything so mundane as work while he finishes his residency."

I frowned at the picture Janette so accurately painted. "You know too much about my family."

"That's what happens when you drag me with you whenever you have to go visit. If only your mom had turned out like your cute little grams."

"But see then, my life would be perfect, and I'd have nothing to whine about."

"Of course. And I'd absolutely hate that," she said dryly and went back to her book.

I put Everett's name in my phone alongside the anonymous number that had called all afternoon, and then I texted him an invitation to Grams's birthday party. I didn't want to go alone and since he was offering his company for the evening . . .

His response dinged back before I put my phone down on the table.

I would love to, he texted,

He didn't even question the nearly two hour drive to Connecticut.

I spent more time getting ready than I'd ever spent in my life for any date—in spite of Janette's warning. A med student would be kind of the perfect boyfriend. He'd understand my time crunches. He'd be able to help with homework. We could study together.

Rebound.

That word kept popping in my head, too. When I was finished slipping into the best little black dress any girl had a right to own and sliding my feet into strappy heels that made me feel tall, I looked in the mirror and squared my shoulders. The dress was perfect, slimming, and sexy without being so over the top, Grams would scowl at me.

Take that, two-timing tool.

Which made my hand halt mid-grab for my clutch purse.

Rebound?

Gah! No. My feelings for Everett had nothing to do with his nefarious roommate. I grabbed the clutch and headed to the front door at the same time the bell rang.

Janette gave me one last look as I reached for the door handle, and her lip lifted in a little half smile. "Whatever you choose, you'll look great choosing it. Have fun at the ball!"

I abandoned the door and smooshed my roommate up in a big hug. "You always say just the right things."

"Even when the logic hurts?"

"Especially when the logic hurts." I swept up the present that sat by the front door and opened the door to meet my date that was anything but logical.

Everett shook me down for information on my family during the entire drive to Hartford. He wanted names and descriptions, ambitions and defeats, topics too sensitive to bring up, political affiliations, religious inclinations.

By the time we arrived, Everett probably knew more about my family than I did. He coasted up the street lined with the cars of guests, who knew what a party meant when that party was being thrown by the Stone family, and ended at the circular drive. "Are you nervous?" I asked.

"Not at all."

"You should be. C'mon." I led him to Grams's door, which was one of those doors designed to accommodate a visit from a giantess. Everett tilted his head back to view the top of it. "Wow. Your Grams is tall, huh?"

I punched him lightly on the shoulder and let myself in to the house.

I clutched Grams's present in one hand and Everett's hand in the other as I wove him around crowds of neighbors and old family friends in search of the one person who could ever induce me to spend time with my family.

"There's the birthday girl!" I said, settling her present near the food table and rising up on my tip-toes to kiss my Grams's cheek. "Aren't you supposed to be shrinking as you get older so I can pretend to be tall around someone?" I asked her.

"Ah, my Andra! I didn't expect you to drive all the way over from school!"

I reclaimed Everett's hand and tugged him closer. "I didn't drive. I got me a chauffeur. Grams meet Everett Covington."

"Covington? That sounds like quite a very lofty family name," Grams said.

Everett put his hand out to shake Grams's. "Sorry to disappoint you, Mrs. Stone, but the sound of lofty and the reality of lofty are very different things."

Grams laughed and shook Everett's hand. He inquired after her tennis game and challenged her to a match sometime in the future, though he agreed she'd beat him soundly since he never played tennis. Satisfaction found its way to my lips as I watched him with her. Had anyone ever done a better job at greeting my grams? No. Not one man in my entire life ever made her laugh within the first moments.

Had any of them ever made her laugh?

I didn't think so.

My brother appeared from around the corner just at that moment. "Did I hear Andy come in?"

"Nathan!" I ran and gave him a hug during which he swept me up and swung me around, as was our custom. This never got old for me and was the only benefit of stunted growth: I'd never get too big for it.

"Where's Mom?" I whispered to him, wondering how long it would be before I had to deal with her.

"Bossing the kitchen staff around," he whispered back.

"And Dad?"

"I don't know. I've been lucky enough to avoid him all night. Or maybe he's avoiding me." Nathan shrugged and gave a meh kind of face. "So who's the guy schmoozing Grams?"

"My friend."

Everett and Grams had worked their way toward us, close enough that Everett caught the tail end of the conversation. "I'm also her accomplice for criminal mischief."

If he had said that around anyone else in my family besides Grams and Nathan, I would have killed him. The last thing I needed was for word to get to my parents about the incident with the police and with Jazzy Dean.

"Crime?" Nathan swung an arm over my shoulder. "Our Andy? Not even a possibility. Which was a huge disappointment during our childhood. She would have been lots more fun if she hadn't been so unbending when it came to rules."

I rolled my eyes and squiggled out from under my brother's arm with the intent of removing Everett from the conversation before it could go any further. But Everett changed the subject. He asked Nathan all about his YouTube channel and his culinary experience and his favorite recipes.

Grams smirked at them and dragged me over with her to greet guests and do the tedious job of being gracious to birthday well-wishers. "If I have to do this, you might as well have to do it with me," she said.

I stayed with Grams for quite a while, long enough that my mom and then my dad found me, and both of them sniffed in disdain about my life choices. Mom was devastated that I no longer dated Greg, as he was from such a nice family and she'd seen some real potential there. Dad was indifferent to my dating situation. He had other issues.

He fixed me with a look that made me feel like a bug pinned to a science fair poster. His slicked back dark hair shone in the warm lights from Grams's antique lamps. The Rogaine and dye job must have been doing their jobs because he actually looked like he wasn't balding and wouldn't be any time soon. "A friend of mine sent me an interesting email," he said.

My breath stuttered in my throat. I didn't encourage him to continue, but he did anyway.

"Yes, it would appear that a certain student at Boston University is in a bit of trouble—enough so that they are considering disciplinary action against this student." His eyes narrowed.

"That's too bad. The student probably didn't even do anything wrong."

A low growl at the back of his throat showed he wasn't all that impressed with my answer. "Andra. What have you done?"

"It's nothing. I'm not in any real trouble."

"That's not what my friend said. He said they were contemplating pulling your scholarship."

This was the problem with having a heart surgeon father who was highly respected and esteemed in the medical world. He knew everyone. Everyone knew him. And they all revered him enough that these same people acted as if they were his personal spies and reported back to him all the details of my life.

"They might be pulling my scholarship," I admitted.

"Andra . . ."

He wanted to yell at me. He wanted to rant and rave and perhaps even throw things. I'd seen him throw tantrums like that before.

But the beauty of a party setting was that he wouldn't make a scene over anything. No one would be allowed to raise voices.

Public parties made family time so much more civil.

"What did you do?" he asked.

"I broke up with my boyfriend."

He snorted softly. "I doubt childish relationships are enough to move university review boards to action."

"They would be if people like Mom were in charge."

He frowned as if uncertain whether I meant the remark as a compliment or an insult. "What did you do?" he asked again.

"I painted his car and then cleaned his car off. It's good as new. No harm, no foul."

A distinguished and geriatric looking man waved to us from across the room. Dad waved, gave a false smile, then said through gritted teeth, "Why is it whenever people say no harm, no foul, someone has usually been harmed, and something always smells foul?"

The geriatric crossed the room and stood in front of us. "Dr.

Stone!" he exclaimed and took my father's hand and pumped it with enthusiasm.

I used the moment to slip away.

Grams must have announced that I'd brought a male friend from Boston; Mom eagle-eyed her way around the guests until she spotted him. She was at his side before I had time to blink. I felt genuinely sorry for Everett but not sorry enough to force myself to join them where I would have to witness the embarrassing things she would say.

Knowing she would say them was bad enough.

I joined Nathan at the food tables.

"Your boyfriend is apparently bilingual," Nathan said as he filled his plate with finger foods that he scowled at before eating. "These are terrible!" he said after popping a little sandwich in his mouth and then spitting it back into his napkin. "Where does Mom find these caterers?"

"Bilingual?" I prompted him back to the conversation he started.

"Yeah, the guy speaks crème brûlée. I think you should marry him."

"I'm not getting married. And I'm too young to get married."

He dropped his napkin on his plate with a shiver of disgust and set it back on the table. "Okay. But if you change your mind and/or ever grow up, which is not the same as grow tall since we all know *that* isn't going to happen for you, I've decided he's the one."

"Right. Because I don't have enough people making decisions about my life."

"Yes, but I'm smarter than the rest of them, and you like me better."

"You don't know I like you better." I took a bite out of one of the finger sandwiches Nathan had already declared inedible, figuring he was too picky so his opinion couldn't count too much. And it was a sandwich. How hard could it be to make a sandwich that tasted good?

Apparently very hard.

I spit the pasty texture into my napkin while Nathan watched with amusement. "I do know you like me better because your other choices are Mom and Dad. I win because my competition is lacking."

He explained how Dad had tried to bribe him to go back to school under the guise of spending quality time with me in Boston. Dad then said he really needed the help because he felt he had no one to look after me, and he worried about me, and proceeded to guilt trip Nathan into making the move.

"So you better not let him hear about painting your ex's truck or I will never hear the end of it," Nathan said.

I widened my eyes and lifted my shoulders.

Nathan grunted at me. "He already knows? Why? You're not Catholic! You don't have to go to confessional!"

I lowered my voice so the people who had come to refill their plates for the sixth time wouldn't overhear. "Do you think I have no sense of self-preservation? Of course I didn't tell him. One of his medical buddies who serves on the board emailed him. The guy has more spies than a small government trying to get their hands on nuclear weaponry."

Nathan fixed me with a determined stare. "I am not moving to Boston to babysit you."

"Good."

We both gave our heads one sharp nod in agreement.

Everett finally showed back up at my side and whispered, "Your mom likes me." He grinned wide.

"Since I make a habit of not liking anything she likes, that's not exactly working in your favor, Everest without an S," I whispered back.

"Maybe not. But it works in yours. She's very glad you're going to Boston University as long as she knows you've got me to look out for you."

Could his grin get any wider?

I laughed at him, shook my head and looped my arm through his in the friendly way I had done a dozen times when he'd gone out with Greg and me to dinner or movies. Only, for some reason, it didn't feel friendly this time as much as it felt intimate. When Everett placed his hand over mine in the crook of his arm, and his thumb traced a small circle over my fingers, my face felt like someone had put it in the oven on broil.

The "Happy Birthday" song began as the lights went out and a cake with a million candles rolled into the room. I had never been so grateful to have lights go out than I felt at that exact moment.

Even my mom's meddling and my sudden hyper awareness of all-things-Everett couldn't keep me from smiling at Grams oohing and aahing over the cake and the candles. She blew hard and the room went dark as she got every last one.

"That's my grams," I said.

"She likes me too, by the way," Everett whispered in my ear.

"Okay. That's one thing in your favor."

One thing totally and completely in his favor.

The fact that my face warmed every time I thought about kissing him the night before was another thing in his favor.

By the time he'd wowed my whole family and the evening was through and he'd driven me home and walked me to the door, I felt a bit of breathlessness. This was something new, something different than anything I'd ever had. This could totally work.

And when he kissed me again and I felt all melty and ridiculous the way I'd heard girls describe but had never experienced for myself until this moment, I couldn't imagine anything more perfect.

My grams once told me that life was made up of millions of little moments, but that there were only a few moments that were actually worth a million. She always said that recognizing the million in one was the most essential part of happiness. According to her, most people overlooked those moments because they were too busy looking to the future and they didn't realize what they'd missed until long after it was gone.

I knew the moment at exactly the moment it happened. The universe snicked into place when his mouth settled softly on mine. He had met my family and walked away unscathed or running in the other direction. He had won over my brother and my grams. He had shown me two of the most perfect days in my life. I felt myself tangling into him more and more the longer we were together.

A flawless, stunning, tangle.

I'd pretty much lost my head and heart to the moment, when my phone rang. It startled me so much that my finger slid over the screen without me thinking of who was calling or why I was answering when the last thing I wanted on the planet was to be interrupted. It wasn't until after I put the phone to my ear and answered a breathy "Hello?" that I realized the word *Dad* had been on the screen.

Everett's mouth dropped to my neck where he lightly traced kisses just behind my ear. I almost dropped the phone.

When my dad's voice came through the speaker, forceful and furious, with a single word, "Andra!" I almost dropped the phone for entirely different reasons.

"Dad?"

Everett backed away from me as if my father had found his way to my porch and had walked in on us kissing goodnight in person.

"I just received another email, Andra." The severe tone felt familiar. How many times had he spoken to me in that same severe tone?

Another email? Another email meant nothing good for me. None of my dad's friends and colleagues ever tattled on me for doing anything well.

"You've lost your scholarship. It's time to come home."

Chapter Six

I didn't go home in the aftermath that followed the board's decision to pull my scholarship. They made me repay tuition for the full year but even then, I stayed at Boston University. With only a semester left before graduation, and with transferring ensuring the addition of other class requirements that would extend the length of time it would take to get a bachelor's degree, I did the only logical thing a girl in my position could do. I got a job and a student loan.

My parents felt the rub of my refusal to go to them for assistance. They acted the part of two people who were delirious with the need to rescue me, when what they were really delirious over was the need to control me.

My brother supported me with thumbs-up icons in texts, and Grams slipped me a few hundred dollars every month.

Everett . . . Everett became a liability.

Time with him took time from studying. My parents' approval of him reminded me of all the reasons he wasn't right for me because, really, had anything they'd ever approved of been right for me?

And that was how I found myself on the shores of the Charles River, sitting in the twilight on a metal fold-up chair, clutching my phone and the wretched message it held on its screen from my new employer at the restaurant.

We need you to come in and work tonight, Kelly is sick.

I felt like shouting to the world, "I'm only one person!" so they would recognize that I could not do everything for everyone.

Instead I looked up at Everett. "I can't do this anymore," I whispered, trying to keep from disturbing the other people listening to an amateur symphony performing at the Hatch Shell. The texts from the restaurant always demanding more hours. The texts from my father insisting I was being stubborn and childish and needed to accept help or I would flunk out of school altogether and shame him before the entire medical world. They shredded my strength and resolve.

Everett's chair squeaked as he leaned my direction, his eyes stayed on the orchestra at the front. "Hm?" he asked.

"I'm sorry. I just . . ." I'd been thinking about homework since we left my apartment to come to this practice—the same homework I'd gotten behind on because my new job waitressing had booked me a double shift when one of the waiters didn't show up. Every note the orchestra played sounded like the death march. I had to keep my grade point average solid and get studying for the MCAT so I could continue with my plan of attending UMASS for med school. The orchestra was a distraction I could not afford.

I shook my head as the finishing notes of Ode to Joy rang through the air. The following applause made me feel queasy. I stood. As the applause quieted and before the next song began, I said, "I just can't."

With that, I fled through the audience, up the jogging path.

Running felt better. Running felt like I was doing something. Running felt like the stresses of losing that scholarship and the financial burdens and familial lecturing that followed would fall away from me if I could just run fast enough.

"Andra!" Everett called from behind.

I squeezed my eyes shut as if such an action would close my ears too. No. I couldn't stop. Couldn't wait for him to catch up. Couldn't explain.

Just had to run.

"Andra!" His feet pounded the jogger path behind me, closing the distance between us.

Crazy? Am I crazy? Is this breakdown I'm having fixable?

I didn't know. My feet beat a steady staccato. The water and boats blurred to one side while the trees, people, cars blurred to the other.

I can't.

Right foot.

I.

Left foot.

Can't.

Right foot.

I.

Left foot.

Can't.

His hand was on my arm, pulling me to a slower pace, creating enough drag that I had no choice but to actually stop.

"Andra . . ." He gulped for breath. "What are you doing?"

I stared at him, feeling the wildness in my movements.

"I need to study."

He blinked as if expecting something else, something more intense, more wrong. "Okay. Let's go study."

"No. Not *let's*. Just *I*. Just one. Just me."

"I don't understand."

"I'm a doctor!" I spit out, not knowing where the tantrum was coming from. "I don't have time to be a girlfriend, too. I need to study or my MCAT score will suck. And because I lost my scholarship, I need to work, which means I don't have time to study and I feel . . . overwhelmed right now."

He was quiet for a long moment, long enough that I would have turned and run away again if he hadn't had a firm grip on my arm. When he spoke again, he did so quietly, but it still startled me enough to jump at the first words. "You don't have to work, you know. You chose that. You had a plan B. You just don't want to follow through with it."

"There is no plan B. No possibility of a plan B. How can you even say that? You've met my family! You know what they're like. They hate the idea of me going to med school. If I take money from them, then I'll have to follow the career paths they chose, and I can't live like that. I thought you understood."

"I'm trying to understand. I'm in all the same classes you are, Andra. I do understand the stress you're under. I just don't see why we can't work on this together."

We had to move off the path so we didn't get run over by a group of evening joggers. His hand stayed on my arm.

I rubbed at my eyebrow, trying to ease the headache that lately always seemed to be there, pounding just over my eye. "I'm just . . . wrung out. And I can't do it anymore. I'm a heart doctor, not a girlfriend."

He tried to smile, tried at a joke to lighten the tension weighing heavy over the both of us. "One could say that a girlfriend is the very best kind of heart doctor."

I tugged my arm from his grasp. He let go without a struggle, as if he sensed how lost the fight really was. "I'm not that kind of heart doctor. I'm sorry." I ran then, faster and harder than I'd ever run in my life.

I didn't look back.

And felt heartless for the shattered look in his eyes as I turned away.

A heart surgeon who broke hearts and who had no heart.

How ironic.

The Second Chamber

Four Years later

Kissing is like drinking salted water: you drink and your thirst increases
—Chinese proverb

Chapter Seven

My phone vibrated, but I resisted the urge to answer it until I was done reading. If it was the hoped-for call, then it would mean that the tenant to the apartment I'd been on the waiting list for had finally vacated the premises.

But I had to finish reading the syllabus. Because the information was so dry and horrible and boring that if I didn't finish it now, I would never find the willpower to go back to it. And to arrive at clinical rotations without having read the syllabus would make me look incompetent, unprepared, and lazy.

But the apartment! My apartment! The one I had drooled over and waited for, and coveted online for over a year was finally going to be mine.

It wasn't just that the stone building was beautiful and covered in ivy and located close enough to the hospital that I could walk, even on the coldest winter days and not feel too badly over it since I wouldn't be outside for very long, but it was also that it was one of the cheapest apartments available in Worcester. Living there would save me several hundred dollars every month.

And that would keep the debt from piling up more than it already was.

The apartment.

And the bigger beauty was that even though it carried one of the cheapest rents, it was also one of the few affordable private apartments in the neighborhood. I could ditch the roommates who ignored personal boundaries and borrowed things like my shampoo and conditioner and razor, and who ignored things like common decency and finished off the last of the milk that I paid for and then never rinsed the glass they used so the bottom was left caked with soured milk that had to be scoured out.

A private, cheap apartment.

And honestly, what kind of woman would even *want* to use another woman's razor? The very idea made my stomach lurch.

My eyes had made it to the bottom of the page but my brain hadn't registered a single word read.

Fine, it's not like you'll be able to focus until you know. I swept my finger over the screen and read the message waiting for me.

Andra, Emily texted. *Just got word. Brad is quitting. He can't handle the idea of rotations and is moving home. He should be gone in two weeks. I told the landlord you were still interested. He usually only rents to guys. But I know he wants to lease it to a serious med student. I told him you didn't even know how to spell the word fun. Keeping fingers crossed!*

I leaned back in my chair and frowned at my screen. The little dig at my personality tempered some of my elation to know the apartment was going to be vacant soon.

I knew how to spell fun. I even knew how to have it when there was time to be spared for such things.

Of course, Emily was just being funny. She thought little quips like that were hilarious and no one escaped her barbed humor.

But I didn't like it.

I sucked in a deep breath and focused on the real message. The apartment!

How nice would it be to not have to hide food in my closet or under my bed or to hide my really expensive spices in my underwear drawer beneath the granny panties that I'd bought specifically to hide things under. No one wanted to touch those monstrosities—not even the evil roommates.

How fabulous would it be to take a shower without the water running cold just as my hair had been freshly shampooed and needed a rinse?

How exquisite would it be to not have to remind roommates of test days and TV volume levels?

Another deep breath—only this one was a sigh of happiness. A place of my own. The one thing every human needed in order to regroup and figure things out. The importance of a personal sanctuary was an often overlooked concept.

I texted Emily back. *Not just still interested, but ready to move this exact minute if he'll let me. Being the beginning of the semester, it couldn't come at a better time!*

Nothing smelled quite as terrible as desperation, but sometimes it was best to explain things as they really were, stench-of-desperation be hanged.

Emily's text chimed in. *He's got a few others waiting, but you've been on the list for such a long time, I'm sure he'll give you preference.*

The good news remained good news all day, so that when Evil-Roommate-Anne finished off the cheesecake my brother had brought me, I didn't really get that mad. Her mutant behavior only served as a reminder of all the many things I would have to be grateful for when I finally moved.

The apartment existing, with its supreme location, could have been very profitable to the owner. But he'd been a med student at UMASS and done his rotations at UMASS Memorial and had bought that apartment when his grandfather died and left him a modest inheritance. As a way for his grandfather's legacy to live on, the man rented the apartment to med students only, charging them a rent that barely covered property taxes for the year. He only considered need-based students, which, in spite of my parents' affluence, was totally me.

The thoughts of the apartment overpowered the base from evil-roommate-Becky's screamo music that night. I went to sleep chanting the words, "Not that much longer, not that much longer . . ."

I woke before the sun and hurried to get ready for the first day of rotations. After two years of text books and classroom lectures, my third year in med school stood as a reward for my hard work and patience. I would finally get to see real patients; not cadavers, school books, or video tutorials. Real, talking, walking, breathing people. First days were the most important. They were the ones that allowed everyone to assess each other and get a grasp of what the rest of rotations held in store. Fueled by nine grain toast and a berry yogurt, I left my apartment. My white lab coat pressed and so white, it glowed as if I was radioactive.

When I'd emailed my preceptor regarding what to expect the first day of rotations, her response had been to make sure I arrived tidy and timely. She said to consider showing up early as my new definition of "on time." Showing up early meant that though I'd likely be kept waiting, no one would be forced to wait for me.

I arrived twenty-eight minutes early, and found I wasn't the only one who'd made that choice. A couple of people from the previous year's study groups came in, laughing about their weekend activities. The group had all bonded during the intense year we spent together, and these two stayed close after the final class grades were posted. I didn't remain best friends with anyone from that group. Splitting my focus for relationships felt like a great way to sidetrack my goals.

I smiled and waved at them. Not wanting to be best friends didn't mean I didn't want to be friends at all. They waved back and seemed genuinely pleased to see me again. But they didn't come to stand with me outside the office where we were supposed to meet for our first day. They herded themselves to the other side of the door and kept their conversations contained inside their tight little circle of two.

All the other students were complete strangers to me, which seemed impossible. Two years of medical school and these people owned barely recognizable faces. Was I incapable of human connections?

Regret bubbled in my stomach. This sort of moment made me truly miss Janette. She lived in Arizona and worked as a nutritionist at a hospital in Phoenix. We emailed and texted and commented on each other's social media, but those things did not replace a living, breathing best friend. As I stared hard at my syllabus and tried to remind myself that there would be time for friendships later, a hand slid across my vision. "Well, well, well. If it isn't Andrea without an E." My entire body froze at words I hadn't heard in a very long time and the voice I hadn't realized I also missed, until that very moment.

"Everest without an S," I whispered, slowly turning to face the direction the hand came from. He looked good. He hadn't gone flabby like several of the guys in med school who kept touch via social media. I took his hand and shook it as if we were introducing ourselves to each other for the first time.

His warm hand in mine brought such a rush of memories, they

almost knocked me over. What was he doing here? Why would he choose to stand with me after what I'd done to him? How did he end up in the same hospital as me for even a moment?

He must have sensed at least part of my confusion because he said, "Transfer student." He put up a hand to stop the protest on my lips. "I know. Transfer students are incredibly rare, but they aren't impossible. It happens sometimes." He pointed to himself as if presenting Exhibit A.

"But you'd always planned on going to Tufts. What would ever make you want to come here?" The question sounded accusatory. I fully realized that these were not the best first words to say to the guy I'd abandoned on the Boston Common years ago.

An apology would have been better, maybe an explanation of how the pressure had finally got to me and I just sort of blew up. I recognized the immaturity of my actions, but could only excuse them because of my legitimate youth at the time—too young to be taking on so much on my own. I stared at him now, wondering if he had limped back to his apartment all those years ago and commiserated with Greg—the other ex in my life—about what a perfect troll of a female I'd turned out to be. Maybe they fantasized about spray painting *troll* on my car like I'd painted *tool* on Greg's truck. Did Everett hate me now? Did he look at me and see all the ways I was undependable and completely fickle?

Thinking of Everett hating me shot pangs of guilt and even more regret through me, enough that I felt sick and dizzy and confused.

"Happy to see me, huh?" he said.

I blinked and sucked in a breath that didn't seem to contain any oxygen. "Of course I'm happy to see you. I'm just surprised." I leaned in to give him a quick hug, partly because I really needed to hang on to something solid or I would pass out from lack of oxygen and partly to cover the fluster in my face.

Someone from behind bumped me with a shoulder, which bounced my head forward a bit and jolted me out of . . . whatever that feeling between flustered and relieved I felt at being in such close proximity to Everett.

"Watch it, Adam," Everett said, giving the guy behind me a good-natured reprimand over the fact that the bump made me pull away from our embrace.

The guy, Adam, gave a light tug on my ponytail. "What? Am I ruining your chances with the ladies?"

I turned around to see who interrupted my reunion with Everett and almost felt like my knees might buckle at the sight of the newcomer. He looked like he'd been designed instead of born, like the rest of us mere mortals. Not one flaw marked the bronzed skin that set off and magnified his blue eyes. His blond hair had that moussed, messy style that seemed to invite female fingers to play in it.

He looked more like a California surfer than he did a New England med student, but he wore the white lab coat that marked him as a student.

I don't know how I reacted when he flashed his confident grin at me. Did I smile back? Did I just stare at him? *Oh please tell me I didn't whimper.* I opened my mouth to try to articulate something beyond a squeak when the physician we would be spending the next five weeks with called our attention to the hallway in front of his office.

With gratitude, I faced forward again. I did not want to face Everett next to me or the Photoshopped man on my other side.

Everett slouched so he could lean over and whisper in my ear. "You're not looking at him anymore. You can close your mouth now, Andra."

My cheeks burned with the knowledge that my mouth *had* gaped open when I first saw Adam. I snapped it closed with a click of my teeth.

Everett chuckled softly next to me, and I was suddenly *not* glad that Everett knew me well enough for this kind of familiarity.

"Don't worry." His whisper tickled my ear again. "Adam has that effect on all the girls. He's a player, and since you have a history with players . . . I thought it fair to warn you."

What? One bad boyfriend decision suddenly counts as a track record? If he intended on making me feel better about momentarily acting like a vapid sorority type, he failed. He might as well have rubber-stamped the word *average* on my forehead. I was not one of *those* girls.

"I don't know what you're talking about." I kept my tone cool. The physician must have said something funny because everyone else laughed. I cast a frantic glance around the group to see if I'd missed anything important, but couldn't really tell. Whatever had been said was clearly amusing, but was it necessary to know?

The physician failed to add follow-up information that would allow those not paying attention to catch up. I had to swallow my pride. "What did he say?" I whispered to the girl to my right. She ignored me like she hadn't heard.

"He said to be nice to your classmates and hospital staff because the people you see around you might be the very people in charge of hiring and firing at hospitals you want to work at in the future," Everett whispered. Was that a reprimand in his words? Was he really trying to make me feel dumb for not paying attention when he'd been the one distracting me?

I mumbled a thanks, determined to pay attention to the attending physician. I already knew how important professional relationships were during the rotations, and no man, not the beautiful one or the teasing one, was going to mess with that.

"I'm sure you all already read the syllabus so you know that I'm Dr. Jonathon Niles. You've already all communicated with your preceptor, Crystal, so I feel certain you're all already familiar with her and require no introductions. We have a busy day ahead of us, so let's get moving."

And move we did.

The first rotation was in geriatrics. I chose this one first at the advice of my father who, albeit grudgingly, resigned himself to the fact that I was going to medical school and nothing he did or said would sway me. He figured if I was joining the profession, then he had better make sure I didn't do anything to smudge the reputation of the four generations of doctors that came before me through the Stone family tree. Since I felt pretty certain I wanted to be a heart surgeon—like my father—he advised me to begin rotations in something that I was definitely not going into. That way, I learned how the hospital, and my role in the hospital, worked in an area that mattered a little less.

That first day, I tried hard to stay visible, to take good notes, to ask intelligent questions, to volunteer when Dr. Niles offered the chance for hands-on work. As I helped, I had my hand patted by several old women, and my backside patted by one old man who winked and waggled his eyebrows at me. Both Adam and Everett laughed at that. Pretty much the entire group got a laugh at my expense. I think even Dr. Niles might have twitched his mouth. The fact that the old man said, "Ni-ce", long and drawled out with appreciation only made the situation that much more horrible.

By the end of the day, I felt like someone had plunged me into ice cold water and then wrung me out with a vicious twist. I went back to gather my belongings when I was joined by Everett and Adam.

Adam was a transfer student, as well. He and Everett were joined at the hip in a way that I didn't really understand and didn't really want to understand.

"Hey," Everett said, "Andrea without an E?"

"Yes, Everest without an S?" I answered without looking at him.

"Some of the class is having a get-together—kind of a get-to-know-each-other kick-off. Want to—"

I couldn't.

Whatever it was, I couldn't.

I could not fall into the trap of Everett and the danger he represented of making me forget myself. I was already thinking of excuses when Adam-the-beautiful said, "You can't invite her."

I startled and shot my head up to meet his gaze. "And why can't he?"

"How old are you? Sixteen? We need to put you on the arrest alert. Are you even legally old enough to be in this hospital without a chaperone?"

"I'm twenty-four." My ear tips went hot.

Everett raised an eyebrow. He knew the lie. My birthday wasn't for another four months. I was only twenty-three.

Adam-the-beautiful with his golden waves and bright blues eyes looked genuinely shocked. "No way! Twenty-four? Really? You're what? Five feet tall?"

"Five three." I felt the petulance in my tone, like a seven year old demanding to be acknowledged as *seven-and-a-half.*

"Huh." Adam eyed me with new interest. "I had you pegged for the doctor's kid . . . a sort of take your daughter to work day thing, but really? You're a full on med student?"

"Is there a reason you're working so hard to insult me?"

I expected him to make a crack on my height again, or maybe something about girls not finishing school—something my father said all the time—but he didn't. Instead, his smile widened and his eyes focused in. "My mistake."

He held my gaze, even when several other students jostled to get around him in the narrow aisle. "Everett still can't invite you to our party."

Like he had any right to say what Everett could or could not do? Like he had any right to determine what *I* would do? His words shook some sense back into me. A pretty boy would just throw off my jam.

"I can—" Everett started to say, but Adam spoke over the top of him.

"He can't because *I'm* inviting you."

I stared at Adam, whose arrogance lost him beauty points. Everett also stared with an anger that gave off actual heat. I snorted. "Does that kind of approach usually work for you?"

Adam blinked and actually twitched his head back a little. He had definitely expected that insulting me and then talking over a person who was obviously already an acquaintance of mine would work for him. That crap might have worked when I stood blinking in my first semester of actual college, but not anymore. He must not have dated many educated women.

The only thing to do at such a bizarre moment was to loop my arm in Everett's and say, "I'm really sorry, Adam. Maybe next time. I've already committed to spending some time with my dear friend, Everett."

Everett's eyes traveled from where our arms linked together to my eyes as if he wasn't quite sure what had just happened. I smiled up at his confused face.

"Right," Everett confirmed, not taking his eyes off of mine. "Her dear friend."

"Oh." Adam also looked confused, but likely because no one had ever turned him down before. "Right. You two knew each other from before then?"

I answered since Everett seemed reluctant to explain our personal connection and situation. "Yes. From before."

Adam waited for more of an explanation, but when I didn't give him one, he shrugged, said, "Oh. Well good for you, Evs, I didn't know you had it in you," and wandered off.

"Evs?" I asked once Adam was out of earshot. "You go by Evs now?"

"Only with Adam, but only because he doesn't care how often I remind him that it isn't my favorite nickname." His eyes trailed back to our arms.

Flushing hot, I jerked my arm from his and took a step back as if he'd been on fire and I was afraid to get burned. "Sorry. I was just trying to get out of a date."

"Yes. You got out of one date and got yourself into another. Score one for team Evs." He grinned at me—a look so *him* and so entirely missed that I couldn't help but smile back.

"Team Evs, huh?"

"It's growing on me. So what time should I pick you up and what's your address?"

Jani, one of the girls from last year's study group said goodbye and waved at me. I waved back and then decided I really did want to know how Everett ended up with a shadow. "So what's the deal with you and the other transfer student?"

Everett nodded. "We were kind of a package deal. His dad is owed a lot of favors in the medical community. I'm his babysitter."

I grunted. "In this modern day, that sort of thing can still happen?"

"What *thing* do you mean? The grown man with an *au pair* or the handshakes reeking of undeserved favors for prominent daddy's boys?"

"When the rest of us have worked hard to get where we are, that sort of thing really—"

"Shh." Everett cut me off since the rant had taken a fairly loud pitch. He took me by the arm and let me out into the hallways and down the stairs to the front entrance. "Those handshakes were made by a few people in this administration. You don't want to condemn too loudly. Where's your car? I'll walk you to it."

I pointed in the direction of my car, and he set us off at a meandering sort of pace, as if he was an old man on his last walk ever. The thought startled me a little in light of the fact that we'd left a hospital filled with old people who might very well never leave. How did geriatric doctors do it? How did they work day in and day out at that end of life when all of biology was working against them?

I frowned and shook off my own morbid thoughts. Doctors existed to give biology a run for its money. "So Adam . . . What's his story?"

"He's a playboy."

When Everett didn't explain any further I said, "Huh. Short story."

"He trifled with someone's daughter at Tufts. He didn't get kicked out so much as he was asked to leave. We were roommates there. When he got transferred, and I expressed a sort of interest in transferring as well, since rotations here will allow more in-depth training and study, they moved us both. Kind of a last shot for him and a new shot for me."

"That's kind of pathetic, you know. Not for you, but for him." We arrived at my car. "And you're okay with this situation?" I asked, surprised at how disappointing it was to be at a place of parting so soon.

He smiled. "It's a good opportunity. And now that I have a date with the elusive Andrea without an E, it's become a great opportunity."

I laughed. "Smooth."

He leaned against my car. "So, you never gave me your address."

"Yeah. About that . . ."

"We had a deal. No give backs." He put his hand on my arm, the barest, softest sort of touch.

His eyes, so open and trusting and familiar, made my brain stutter on the words I meant to say.

We stood there for what seemed like forever, our eyes locked, our skin connected by his hand on my arm. "So what's party dress code?" I asked, pulling away, knowing that if I allowed myself to stay exactly as we were, I'd do something impulsive and not smart. How long had it been since I'd felt the basic human contact of something as simple as an embrace?

Too long.

"Casual. Jeans. Shirt. Shoes. Socks. Actually, socks are probably optional, but it's gross not to wear them, so you totally should."

I pulled out my car keys from my bag. "Huh? Never would've pegged you for an anti-sock guy. I'll text you my address. What time?" I looked back at him to find him staring.

"I've missed you, Andra Stone."

Everett moved closer to me—completely invading my personal space. The warmth of his energy made my heart kick up the tempo a notch or two. Had he asked me a question? Said something? Oh, that's right. "Missed me?" I said to prove I was listening.

"*So* missed you. And I'm glad you changed your mind about accepting a date with my narcissistic roommate."

I growled at him. "Hey! I'll have you know that I didn't have to change my mind about anything. I had my mind made up from the beginning."

"I saw the way you looked at him." He was still in my space and it felt like he was closing in.

Was it a hot day outside? Was there too much humidity?

"Looking doesn't mean anything. Appreciating a piece of art in a museum doesn't mean you're going to stick it in your handbag and haul it home."

"Oh, I know. And I'd feel a little hurt by the whole thing except you looked at me in kinda the same way. Maybe, Andrea without an E . . ." He hefted his messenger bag strap over his shoulder and settled his gaze so firmly on me that I couldn't deny looking at him in the same way. "Maybe you missed me, too."

He leaned in like he might kiss me. I stiffened, not sure what to do, but the lean blew past me as he scooted by and on down the road.

I exhaled a deep breath I hadn't realized I'd been holding and was surprised to find that I felt shaky. "Punk," I muttered when he was far enough to be out of ear shot.

The funny thing was that even though I felt certain he hadn't heard me, I still felt like he was laughing somewhere about it.

"Total punk," I said again.

How could he do that to me? Everett Covington always

managed to cut me open and carefully carve out all the feelings I kept tucked away with the skill and precision of a master surgeon.

And I had a date with him

Chapter Eight

Getting ready for my date became the first hurtle to jump. Evil-roommate-Becky occupied the bathroom.

"Becky?" My knuckles thumped the peeled paint of the door. "I need the bathroom. I have to get ready." I called through the wooden door that was so scratched up it appeared to have been through many such conflicts with evil roommates.

"I'm in the tub!" she called back. The noise from her tablet betrayed the fact that she wasn't just in the tub, she was in the tub *and* binge watching the TV series *Gossip Girl*.

"But I really need to get ready. I'll be in and out again in less than fifteen minutes. I promise."

She gave no reply.

I thumped my knuckles against the door again. "Becky? Please?"

At the sound of water draining through the pipes, the tension in my shoulders released and I closed my eyes in silent gratitude. Maybe I'd been wrong about Becky. Maybe she wasn't evil.

I hurried to my bedroom, stepped out of my professional clothes, taking great care to hang the lab coat and smooth it down so it didn't wrinkle in my closet, and slipped on a robe, hastily tying the sash at my waist. I grabbed my toiletry kit from the hiding place behind a stack of medical books and trotted back to the bathroom, expecting to see the door open and light from the bathroom window spilling into the hallway.

The dark hallway provided the first clue.

I frowned, stepped back up to the closed door, and pressed my ear against the wood. Was that the sound of . . . "Becky!" I called and thumped some more.

"What do you want now?"

"I thought you were getting out. I heard the water draining."

"No, I'm not getting out. I told you I was in the tub. The water just got cold. I needed to refill it." She must have turned up the volume because the voices from the TV show became suddenly louder.

"Are you serious?" I called, even knowing she could never hear me over the noise of her speakers and the water running. Why did her actions surprise me? She was evil-roommate-Becky. Of course she was serious.

Thinking thoughts that were less than charitable, I used the kitchen sink to wash my face and brush my teeth. Since washing my hair had been yanked from the equation, I twisted it back into a sloppy up-do that I knew would look nice and hide the fact that my hair hadn't been washed for a couple days.

The truth was that I'd planned on doing exactly what evil-roommate-Becky was doing. I figured spending the evening after my first day of clinicals in a tub, soaking and studying, would be relaxing.

And here I was going out, not relaxing at all.

What is the point of going out?

The question plagued me like liver spots plagued the old guy who'd man-handled me earlier that day.

Dr. Niles and Dr. Liechty stressed several times throughout the day the importance of making relationships and forging friendships with our fellow students and with the hospital staff, but relationships didn't mean dating. Dating complicated everything. Complications were . . . well, complicated.

Could I handle complicated?

I didn't know.

But I continued through the process of getting ready anyway. Because really, going out spared me the anguish of hating evil-roommate-Becky for being in the bathtub all night. This way, I would only be faced with despising her for the short time it took me to get ready.

Leaving the apartment was the absolute best gift I could give myself.

Soon, I would be able to luxuriate in having my own space in my own apartment where there would be no knuckle-thumping on doors. There would be no cold-water showers. There would be no discovering someone drank all my milk when I wanted a bowl of cereal. Soon, I would have the apartment of my dreams: one not inhabited by anyone else.

All I had to do was survive the next few days or weeks. There was a light at the end of this tunnel. The light wasn't a train and the tunnel wasn't so long that it felt impossible.

The doorbell gave a pathetic squawk, alerting me to the fact that someone stood on my front porch. Everett was a little early—perfect. Getting out faster was perfect.

"Your bell sounded like I twisted its arm behind its back when I rang it," Everett announced as soon as I opened the door.

"Yeah. It does that." I shrugged and grabbed my pocketbook from the side table, not daring to leave it where roommates might get hold of it.

"No, seriously." Everett shot a parting look to the doorbell and then reached out and turned the knob that buzzed it again. "I don't think I've ever had to twist a bell before, and did you hear that noise it made?"

I nodded and scooted him forward down the sidewalk.

"It was almost like it cried *uncle* while sobbing big, fat tears. I actually feel guilty for inflicting pain on a doorbell. How can you stand it? I'd clip the wires and put a sign up telling people to knock. Listening to that thing cry and whine at me anytime someone came to visit would give me a case of anxiety."

I laughed. "The bell is such a small thing in comparison to the people who do not just come to visit, but live there permanently."

"Bad roommates?" he asked.

"Let's just say that I either need to hire an exorcist or move out."

"Sorry."

"Just get me out of here."

He draped an arm over my shoulder and walked me out to the car. "That, I can do."

I wasn't uncomfortable under the weight of his arm. I wasn't uncomfortable in his presence. We fell into step, not just there on the sidewalk leading to his car parked on the road, but mentally, emotionally . . . like no time had passed.

I felt grossly uncomfortable with how comfortable he made me feel.

Which made no sense at all.

Once in his car and heading to wherever the enigmatic get-together was located, I turned in my seat. "So tell me the deal with the troll who thinks that insults are the same things as pick-up lines."

Everett shrugged. "Not much to tell really. Not more than I've already told you anyway."

"There has to be something more. After all, you transferred schools. That doesn't happen very often."

Everett took his eyes off the road for a moment longer than would be considered safe and locked his gaze on mine.

I froze under the intensity of his stare, hot shivers coursing under my skin.

He focused back on the road, releasing me from a moment that was . . . whatever it was.

"Let's just say I had incentive to make the transfer."

Did he transfer for me?

No.

Of course not.

How narcissistic could I possibly be to make that assumption? I deleted the thought almost as immediately as it entered my head.

He couldn't have made such a huge change and moved away from colleagues who knew him, who could help him climb the political mountain that comes with medical school, who could talk him up to other colleagues who could give him preferential treatment in placement at a hospital of his choice.

"I actually transferred at the advice of a brilliant doctor who has since moved into administration. She told me that a true surgeon of the heart always follows his heart."

"Sounds like an old proverb."

"Miss Pearl *is* Chinese . . . well, of Chinese heritage anyway. She almost insisted I make the transfer. She all but packed my bags for me. She promised me that my every happiness depended on my transfer."

He turned the car onto the freeway.

"She sounds more like a fortune teller than a medical doctor," I said, noting the direction we traveled seemed far too out of the way to be an intimate get-together among our classmates. "Who picked the location of your party?" I asked.

Everett sneaked a little apologetic side grin at me. "We're not going to the party."

"What?" I straightened in my seat. "I thought the party was the whole point of this evening, to get to know each other and make friends with our classmates so that we were all on the same team. Isn't that what Dr. Niles wanted from us?"

His fingers tightened on the steering wheel, the first sign that I'd punched a hole through his confidence. "I've made the mistake of letting a roommate cozy up to you before I gave myself a sporting chance. I just wanted to . . ." he fumbled for the right words, ". . . hit the reset button."

When I dropped my head to the side and raised my hands palms-up in question, he started again. "Andra, you have to know that I like you, that you're important to me, that you are all I've thought about when I allowed myself to consider dating again. When Miss Pearl asked me if I had anyone in my life, anyone special, I couldn't help myself. I blabbed all about you and how great you are—how you inspire me with the way you handle parents who are less than supportive, how you help your fellow classmates—even when teachers graded on a scale and your classmates were technically your competition. And you never even complained if they managed to score higher than you on exams. You congratulated them. You knuckle-bumped them and encouraged them with the next new hard concept that they would never understand without you there, explaining and mentoring. And I know I'm rambling . . . and maybe that's because you're a captive in my car and I feel like I might never get this chance again, but I wanted to start over, reset—even if that means just being friends. I'd rather be miserable with you in my life, than lost without you."

He finally stopped, whether to breathe or whether he just ran out of things to say, I didn't know. Had Everett ever said so many words all at once?

I'm not sure what my reaction was. I felt overly warm but a little bit cold, too. I shivered. Was I too cold? Maybe I was coming down with something. Hospitals were terrible places to work when my immune system was down due to lack of sleep.

Wait.

What am I thinking?

Everett was in the driver's seat, stripping down to his soul for me, and I was thinking about colds?

"So?" Everett prodded when it became obvious that a lamppost was more likely to give a response than me.

"Everett, I . . ."

"I know. You're not looking for a relationship, but what about a reset on the friendship button? I won't push. I won't prod. I won't kiss."

That startled me out of the shock he'd put me into. No. I wasn't cold. Too hot. It was definitely too hot. "No kissing?" I tried at a laugh that sounded awkward and jittery. "You say that as though kissing is a bad thing."

The look he gave me would have murdered Frosty the Snowman into nothing but a hiss of steam. My stomach wobbled a little as he said, "I'm not kissing you again until you kiss me. But if you kiss me, you won't be sorry. I promise."

Why did that feel like a magnificent promise? It really was too hot in the car. Before I could respond, he said, "So are we on?"

"For a kiss?" I kind of totally hoped that was what he meant.

"For a reset. I want to be your friend. I want to help you study and take notes and be there when geriatric men with excellent taste make passes at you. Can we reset?"

I nodded, not really certain what I was agreeing to. He'd been a little all over the place, and he was right about me being captive in his car. It wasn't like I could walk away from the bizarre and uncomfortable conversation.

It also wasn't like I wanted to.

"Yeesss." I drew the word out slowly, the gentle ssssss of a teakettle telling its preparer that it was ready. "A reset is a good idea."

We went to a late-night diner, found a cozy sort of booth, ordered ice cream, discussed our varying experiences in medical school, compared professors and methods, and lamented over the tests that nearly toppled us over the edge into the chasm of insanity.

Everett politely missed the chance to bring up the break down I'd already experienced with him as my only witness.

He told me about Miss Pearl, who'd apparently imparted

all kinds of fabulous wisdom, and who had steered him toward pediatric medicine.

I told him how I'd survived on my own terms, without my father's help, but with the occasional monetary gifts from Grams.

He asked after Grams and her health, he asked about Nathan's life and mentioned he kept up on Nathan's career via internet stalking.

I asked after his sisters and found that his oldest sister, Riley had become district attorney and that Hazel, the sister just older than him, had started a profitable social good company that made children's toys. He explained their successes with a sort of sigh in his voice.

"What?" I asked. "You're not happy for them?"

"Sure, I'm happy for them. My sisters are great. It's just a little tough to compete."

I squinted at him as if squinting would help me see him better. When it didn't, I took a bite of melty vanilla ice cream that had frothed into a hot fudge soup. "Why do you feel like you're competing with your sisters? You're as successful as they are."

He took a bite of his ice cream too, as if he needed that moment to try and figure out the best way to explain his family. I felt bad that it had never occurred to me to ask before. With all those study groups and all those times I'd been in his apartment while Greg and I dated, and all the classes we shared, I never bothered to look deeper than the medical student.

"Compete is maybe the wrong word," he finally said. "I kind of wish our relationships were more like you with your brother. You guys are pretty solid."

"Well, when you have to join forces to battle the foolishness of parents, your only choice is to stick together."

"Exactly. My sisters never had to join forces with me. They have my mother's total and complete attention at all times."

This news interested me a great deal and pinged a little place in my own heart. Disinterested parents killed enthusiasm for pretty much everything. The fact that both Everett and I dealt with such a thing and still strove for greater prospects in our lives made me feel a kinship to him I hadn't known could exist with anyone besides my own brother.

"What's the deal with your mom then?" I asked.

"Feminist, the bad kind, not the good kind. She's the sort of feminist who is so worried about making sure women have rights that she practices a bizarre reversal of sexism. According to her, men are slothful, lazy, unintelligent creatures who are only interested in sex and video games."

"Ouch."

He stirred his ice cream soup some more. "It's not that big of a deal—more frustrating than anything. My mom was thrilled to get two daughters and less-than-thrilled about being handed a son with her third child. She spent our lives making sure her daughters had opportunities."

"And you?"

He grinned. "She spent my life making sure I had lots of video games."

I wanted to say *ouch* again, to let him know that I felt the sting in that kind of displacement in your own family, especially when you knew you were capable of more than they believed. But I didn't. We didn't really have to say all that. Because he'd met my parents. He already knew I understood.

The evening had been relaxing, filled with genuine friendship, and when it was all over and Everett dropped me off back at my apartment, he only smiled at me, gave me a quick hug and said, "See you tomorrow, Andrea without an E."

He was down the stairs and to his car before I could say, "Goodnight, Everest without an S."

He hadn't tried to kiss me. The elimination of that sort of physical-contact-obligation freed up the entire situation to be something wonderful and different. It allowed Everett and me to be genuine friends, instead of being a part of an awkward couple situation. Having Everett and our friendship *reset* would be sort of like getting Janette back in my life.

Everett's quick-on-his-feet thinking and his cool level head indicated that he'd be a fabulous doctor, which meant I had the world's best study buddy. I took a deep breath as I watched him drive away.

I floated up the last few steps, the smile sliding off my face with each one. Noise vibrated through the front door. Noise and *smell*.

I opened the door to a cloud of cigarette smoke that tumbled out of my living room and into the nighttime air, as if escaping some unexplainable horror. Evil-roommate-Becky and Evil-Roommate-Anne had decided to host a party without asking. A party that ignored our landlord's insistence that there be no smoking and no pets in the apartment.

The parrot that swooped through the living room and over my head violated the no pets rule.

"Shut the door!" Evil-Roommate-Anne shouted. Out of sheer shock, I dumbly obeyed her ordered and slammed the door shut, locking myself in with the smoke and the bird that hadn't managed to flee the crime scene.

The bird landed on an old coat rack that was part of the *furnished* in the advertised furnished apartment, squawked, and squirted a white stream from under its tail feathers onto the floor.

"What is this?" I asked over the music thumping so hard in my chest, it felt like arrhythmia.

"Parrot," Evil-roommate-Becky slurred. She'd been drinking too. Weren't we all a little too old for this college party scene?

"I see that it's a parrot," I shot back. "What is it doing here?"

"It's Leon's service animal," Evil-Roommate-Anne said in a slur that easily matched Becky's.

I didn't know Leon, didn't *want* to know Leon, didn't want to deal with the crazy unfolding in my own apartment. "Clean that up." I pointed to the parrot poop swirling down the wood pole of the coat rack. "And you'd both better hope you can figure out a way to get rid of the cigarette smoke because I am *not* going to die of lung cancer for the two of you! I mean it! Get rid of it now!" I stomped to my bedroom but not before I heard Evil-roommate-Becky say, "She's the Hoover vacuum of our living arrangements. She sucks the fun out of everything."

I opened the door to my bedroom, slipped inside, and slammed it closed again before the smoke could follow me inside. A slight haze hung lifeless and yellow in my room, so I stuffed a towel in the crack under the door and opened my window to let real air inside.

My grandfather had died from lung cancer. Nothing infuriated me more than someone committing slow suicide and trying to take me with them to the grave. Working in the health industry gave me greater appreciation for my health and a stronger desire to not be like the patients filling the beds at the hospital.

I had to get out of this disaster of an apartment,

Now.

I had to get out now.

I checked my phone to see if Emily had written anything more regarding the only thing that would save me from committing homicide.

She hadn't. I went to sleep with noise cancellation headphones and the chant *just a little while longer* on my mental playlist.

Chapter Nine

It had been a week since my date with Everett. In that week, I'd actually managed to get on friendly terms with pretty much everyone I worked with. Well, everyone except Adam who had taken to ignoring me once he realized I wasn't interested in him. Adam had a problem being late to everything and also had a habit of disappearing whenever anyone looked for him. It was actually as I was looking for him so I could have him meet Dr. Niles that I heard a commotion come from one of the rooms. I peeked in to see a full on disaster in progress.

"I can't do this! I can't do this!" Alyssa said, her voice rising in pitch until I thought she might actually scream.

Not that she didn't have just cause. Mrs. Bennion had just vomited back up her pain pills all over Alyssa's white lab coat and stethoscope while Alyssa had been listening to her lungs. Flecks of red vomit clung to strands of Alyssa's red hair.

At least it matched.

But Alyssa wasn't the only one upset by the situation. Ninety-two-year-old Mrs. Bennion sobbed, the stain of red from the afternoon's gelatin side dish seeping into the front of her hospital gown. And her big silent tears rolled down into her mouth as she wept.

Alyssa totally needed a hug, but I was not about to give her one while she was covered in bodily fluids. "You're okay," I told her. "You absolutely *can* do this, but you need to go clean yourself up first. I'll take care of Mrs. Bennion." The old woman, whose big, sad, crying eyes were enough to make me want to begin crying as well, also needed a hug, but I had no intentions of giving her one either, not with her gown soaked like it was.

The nurses were nowhere to be seen, but I called one to Mrs. Bennion's room and then pulled several towels out of the dispenser and ran them under warm water. There was nothing to do except ease Mrs. Bennion's discomfort, and the only way to do that was to clean her up as well as possible until the nurses came to change her clothing and bedding. I gently wiped her face with the warm, wet paper towels which seemed to be enough to get the tears to stop.

Dorothy Bennion had come in for pneumonia. She preferred people to refer to her as Mrs. Bennion, even though she was a widow of nearly thirty years. My rounds put her into part of my daily routine, checking her lungs and other vitals, gauging her improvement. Pneumonia was always something that could quickly get out of hand if left unchecked, and in a woman of her age, it had been truly severe before she came to the hospital. Her body had gone septic. She had a kidney infection, bladder infection, and sinus infection on top of her double-pneumonia.

Her temperature and lungs had to be carefully monitored to make sure the many infections didn't get away from us. And while I took her vitals and tracked her progress back to health, I asked her questions and found out about her life.

At her age, she'd outlived her parents, siblings, spouse, many of her friends, several of her children and even some of her grandchildren and great grandchildren.

Dorothy Bennion had lived a long time, and, vomit in her hair or no, she was an amazing woman.

"Those pain medicines always make me sick," she said. "And now I've made a mess. I'm just a mess."

I mentally went through her list of prescriptions as I cleaned her face. "No. You're not a mess. *Messy* maybe, but that's not the same thing. You're doing fine, Mrs. Bennion. Just fine. Your lungs sound healthy and you'll be out of here and sky-diving in no time."

She actually smiled. "Yeah, right. I wouldn't have gone sky diving even when I was a girl. I never could understand why a person would leap from an airplane that wasn't going to crash."

Her raspy voice sounded like she had a tickle in her throat that needed to be cleared away. Without her teeth in, her gummed words slushed a little like Evil-roommate-Becky's when she'd been drinking.

We talked until the nurses showed up to change her.

I patted Mrs. Bennion's hand. "We'll get you some different pain pills—ones that won't make you sick."

"Tell that poor girl I'm sorry," Mrs. Bennion looked properly ashamed of what had happened.

"Don't give it another thought. She's fine."

"She won't want to be a doctor anymore with things like that happening."

Again, I assured her Alyssa was fine and moved out of the way so the nurses could take care of the clean-up.

"That was a total lie, you know," Everett, who had been listening at the door, said.

"What?"

"Alyssa's freaking out in the bathroom. She's far from fine right now."

I sighed, long and low and stopped to use the counter at the nurse's station to make some notes regarding the incident. "It's a lie, but if I told her that Alyssa was probably having a break down in the ladies room, Mrs. Bennion would feel bad. Would you have wanted me to tell the truth?"

"You have a really great bedside manner. That's something you can't learn from a textbook." He bumped my shoulder, making me miswrite in my notes. I scowled up at him, but he was grinning, so he clearly didn't care about my scowl. "I'm impressed, Andrea without an E. I've never seen anyone make the kind lie actually seem genuinely kind before."

I didn't see what there was to be all that impressed by and didn't really know what he meant by *kind lie*. An old woman was in serious distress and a young med student was having a breakdown. What else could have been done in such a situation? "Don't be too impressed. Everyone has breakdown days. It'll likely be me next time." He already knew about my breakdown days. I checked the time on my phone and let out a yelp. "I'm falling behind, and I still haven't found your worthless roommate. Gotta go. See you, Everest."

"Andra?"

I turned.

"The worthless roommate is in the cafeteria."

I saluted. "Thanks for the tip!" I headed to the elevators. The cafeteria? Was he usually in the cafeteria when he ditched out of his responsibilities? How had this guy managed to pass exams?

How would he manage to pass his secondary exams if he was always living his med student life as a no-show?

Adam was in the cafeteria all right, leaning against the counter and flirting with the cashier who didn't look old enough to be legal. Not that I was in a position to be critical of such things. I didn't look old enough to be legal, either.

"Dr. Niles is looking for you!" I called out.

He jumped like he'd been caught shop-lifting. "Oh. Hey, Andra. I'm just helping . . ." he fumbled for the girl's name.

"Kristin," the girl supplied and then scowled at me like it was my fault the guy couldn't remember her name.

"I don't actually care what you're doing. I only came to tell you that Dr. Niles is looking for you." How did Everett get saddled with this ridiculous excuse for a med student as a roommate?

"Gotta go. Doctor stuff." Adam actually winked at the girl as if he'd said something terribly clever or important when all he did was trivialize the entire medical profession.

He fell into step beside me and let out a huge groan of frustration. "Third year totally sucks, don't you think?"

"How would you know? You haven't been around for most of it. No one can ever find you."

Adam either had the intelligence of a slug or he purposely chose to misinterpret my meaning because he said, "That's just it. Everyone here is always looking for me, telling me what to do, telling me what time to wake up, dismissing me for the night only when *they* feel like it. And crap totally rolls downhill. I have never been shouted at so much in my life. The resident has a bad day, he yells at me. The preceptor has a bad day, she yells at me. The nurse has a bad day, she yells at me. The patients have a bad day, they sit on their sagging, geriatric bedsores and yell at *who*? You guessed it. Me! I'm so sick of it. I keep waiting for the janitor to take a shot at me."

"I'm sorry that's been your experience. I haven't been yelled at by anyone yet, though it'll probably happen. It's a stressful job, and they need us to be accountable and readily available. This is where we prove we can be doctors trusted with people's lives, not just students who need to be babysat."

He squinted his eyes at me. "No one has yelled at you?"

"Nope." I smiled and hoped what I was about to say next would clue him in a little. "I work hard to never give them a reason to. If you do your job and are available when they need you, it'll probably go better for you."

"No wonder Evs is so in love with you."

"Everett is not in love with me. We're just friends."

"Huh. If that's true, then you should go out with *me* sometime."

I stopped in the hallway, for a moment forgetting that Dr. Niles wanted us immediately, and gaped full on at Adam's brazen behavior. "Me not dating Everett does not make you an attractive option. Let's keep things professional, shall we?"

"That's why nobody ever yells at you. You're a stick in the mud. Sticks never get in trouble."

I didn't know why the comment hurt my feelings, but it did. I wanted to reply, to explain that my personality rocked in the most fun-filled way possible, but didn't know if that was true or not. Emily, the girl getting me the apartment, seemed to think *fun* didn't exist in my vocabulary. Either way, I could sleep at night being me. I would never be able to live with myself if my actions and attitudes mirrored Adam's. I stomped off instead of answering. Dr. Niles was waiting and would be irritated enough at the length of time it took me to find Adam. Adam's earlier rant carried some truth. The thing about being a medical student was that nothing you did was ever fast enough. You could be ten minutes early and someone might still insist you were late.

Dr. Niles checked his watch when we entered his office. "You're late, Stone."

"Yes, sir. I know," I said. Explaining that it took me that long to find Adam would have been useless. Dr. Niles likely already knew that's what I was doing. And explaining the situation just made me look like a tattletale who couldn't take responsibility for anything. I'd seen enough unprofessional people in the short rotation week in the geriatric department to know I did not want to emulate any of them in any way.

Dr. Niles nodded as if understanding my situation. We both paused for a moment to allow Adam time to step forward and also take responsibility. Big surprise that he didn't. So we got to work on what turned out to be a long day. I kept notes on each patient—writing down everything I learned about them. When we were finally released to go home for the day, I considered that Adam had been right about that part, too. We left when we were told. We arrived when we were told. Our lives no longer belonged to us.

But we knew all of that going into the profession. Complaining only served to make us look stupid. Besides, I liked the work and didn't mind the schedule. Each new patient offered me a chance to take my knowledge from big picture to detail work. I tucked my notebook into my bag, kind of looking forward to going home later on when they finally released me for the day. Researching some of the patients' conditions would help me understand better how to serve them while doing rounds.

But the time to leave for home didn't come soon. I was asked to intubate a patient to prep him for surgery. While checking the cart to make sure the ventilator and anesthesia equipment were all prepped and ready to go, Everett entered the room with Shara, the anesthesiologist.

"I was sent to help," Everett announced.

"Great." I moved to the side to allow them room to wheel in the patient. "Everything looks good," I informed Shara as she looked over my work. "There aren't any leaks in the gas delivery system and the backup systems and fail safes are all functioning properly."

"Fabulous. Good job, Andra," she said.

I felt a great deal of pride in knowing I set the operating room up accurately.

"New necklace?" Everett asked.

I touched the place where the diamond heart pendant hung at my collarbone. "Yes. A graduation gift from Grams. It's a family heirloom. My great grandfather gave it to my great grandmother when he graduated from medical school to thank her for helping him get through it."

Everett held the laryngoscope in his left hand and shot a quick smirk at me. "A heart diamond . . . . Fitting for a woman who wants to be a heart surgeon."

I flashed him a smile back. "Yes, it is. As soon as she gave it to me, I realized I'd never actually owned anything that meant so much to me." I opened the patient's mouth and tilted his head back. We both focused on the task at hand instead of idle chit chat, but every now and again, Everett's gaze fell on me in a way that warmed me.

Dr. Miles had come in to monitor our work. "Advance the laryngoscope further into the vallecula."

Everett did as directed.

"Nicely done," Dr. Niles said.

The praise, so seldom received, made both of us stand a little taller.

We celebrated the good end to a long day by going to dinner with a few other students. One of them, Tamara, spent half the night smiling too wide at Everett and glaring too hard at me. Adam joined the group unexpectedly halfway through the meal. He plopped himself down next to me and scooted his chair close enough to make Everett do the glaring. During the dinner, I reacquainted myself with people who'd been in my study groups at varying times over the past two years. Jason, Charles, Angie, Frank, Tamara, and Samuel. As we all laughed and compared notes on patients, nurses, and doctors, I realized what I'd been missing out by not allowing myself to socialize with everyone. I'd been mistaken in thinking I didn't have time for people. I had missed real human relationships.

With dinner winding down, Tamara fake-yawned and checked the time on her phone. "Oh! Look how late!"

"Yeah guys. It's definitely time to hit the sack. I was on my feet all day and need to sleep," Everett agreed.

"I'm on your side. Sleeping sounds like a great idea," Tamara agreed. "Hey, Evs, will you take me home? I'm going to need a ride."

Everett's slight jolt showed how her question took him by surprise. "Um . . . Right." He shot a glance my direction as if asking for advice or help. But what could I say? Tell him he wasn't allowed to take other girls home because the very idea sent my insides into spin cycle?

We'd reset on friendship. He promised not to kiss me. I didn't own him.

"Sure," He said when I failed to give him any advice one way or another. "Sure. I'll take you home. Andra, do you need a ride too? Anyone else?" He added the *anyone else* as an afterthought.

"I have my car," I said, declining the offer of a ride and feeling not very happy about it. My not getting a ride from him meant that the all-too-interested Tamara would be alone with Everett in his car.

I tried not to let myself ponder too deeply as to why that bothered me.

Before everyone dispersed to their various destinations, Everett tugged my arm and pulled me into a hug.

"I thought we were just resetting the friendship, not anything else," I said.

I felt his mouth move against my ear in a way that made me imagine him smiling. "This is just a friendly hug goodbye to someone who can intubate a patient like a pro."

I laughed, squeezed him back, and tried to not imagine kissing him. Tamara would definitely not like that, and I had to work with her for the next two years. I also had to work with Everett and kissing complicated everything, even if I did like kissing, even if I did like kissing Everett better than I'd liked kissing anyone.

I drove home feeling annoyed and uncertain as to where all that annoyance came from.

Emily texted me to let me know it would be a little longer on the apartment I wanted.

The evil roommates were having another party.

The next two weeks were filled with days too busy to worry about social activities or evil roommates. Between keeping notes on the patients assigned to me and studying all that ailed those patients so I could drill from big picture to details, more than enough existed to occupy my attention.

Although Everett stayed busy as well, I noted that Tamara worked hard to keep him even busier. She invited him out several times, and Everett had gone with her. Part of me said it was because he was too nice to say no. Part of me said it didn't matter since he was only my friend, and I'd been the one to break things off with him after all. Another part of me felt nothing but animosity toward Tamara and irritation toward Everett for not saying no to her.

To rub salt into the wound, Adam popped up everywhere I was. He kept asking questions about things I liked and my family. He actually tried to be helpful when we were assigned to work together. He asked me out and asked me out and asked me out.

He must have worn me down because I finally agreed to go to a concert of one of my favorite bands: Remember the Ladies. The concert was several weeks away, but once I accepted, Adam talked nonstop about how much fun we would have and how great the night was going to be. I almost regretted agreeing.

In spite of that, things were going well. Third year really did feel like a payoff year. This was what I'd trained for, what I'd wanted while doing Pre-med at Boston. Working on real live people to make those lives better. I learned not just about what ailed my patients, but I learned about their lives, their families, their dreams, their fears. Knowing them personally made it easier to want to do my best for them.

And then everything changed.

It started when Mrs. Bennion went from doing well to not doing well.

And then, when I went in one morning, Dr. Niles pulled me aside.

"I wanted to be the one to tell you before anyone else could. I thought you should hear it from me since I know you've taken a particular interest in her . . ."

"Tell me, sir?"

He cleared his throat, leaned on the side of his desk, and tightened his lips together before finally telling me the news.

Mrs. Bennion died.

"I didn't say goodbye." The words were foolish, infantile, especially coming from someone working on becoming a doctor, but they fell out of my mouth anyway.

Foolish words were often the exhaust of great shock.

Dr. Niles didn't chastise me for saying something foolish. Instead he leaned forward from his desk. "You're a hard worker and a smart woman, Andra Stone. You will be a great doctor someday. I've no doubt you will save many lives and make them better while you're saving them. But you can't save them all. This is going to be hard to hear, but you need to hear it, and hear it from someone who has your best interest at heart. Do not allow yourself to get too close to your patients. Their lives have value and meaning, but they can't get personal to you, especially in the geriatric unit. People die, and you lose your objective ability to save them if your heart is bleeding out all over the surgery floor. Do you understand?"

I nodded, feeling numb from my heart bleeding out all over his office floor.

I understood, but I hated it.

I agreed with him, but almost hated him for imparting this horrible advice.

A friend.

I needed a friend.

Not just someone who was a colleague, mentor, or teacher. I needed a real friend, someone who knew Mrs. Bennion and who knew me and who could maybe plug up some of the holes in my leaky, traitorous heart.

Only one name, only one face, only one person could possibly be that friend for me. I fled Dr. Niles' office as soon as he felt I was composed enough to carry on with my duties. Everett usually made rounds at this time of day and so I went to where he would most likely be found.

But he wasn't there. He wasn't anywhere, no matter how hard I looked. One of the residents told me he'd gone home early due to an emergency. I moved to text him, to tell him to come back and handle my emergency too, but my fingers never swiped the phone on. Instead they slipped it back into my pocket.

I would have to handle Mrs. Bennion's death like an adult.

No. I would have to do better than that.

Like a doctor.

Chapter Ten

I took a deep breath before opening my front door once I arrived home. The entire day had been sort of awful. I needed some peace and hoped that my home would provide me that peace. "They won't be that bad today. They won't be that bad today. They won't be . . ." I opened the door.

"I'm sorry, Andra!" Evil-Roommate-Anne said before I even got the door closed.

"Sorry?"

"I told Becky to stay out of your room."

"Which should have been easy to do since it was locked," I said, feeling an intense wariness I've never had with my roommates, evil or not.

"I'm sure it wasn't locked." she said but looked guilty enough to verify that they had forced their way into my room in spite of the fact that it was, in truth, locked.

I didn't argue the point, not when I needed to know the bigger picture problem as to what exactly Evil-Roommate-Anne meant when she decided to apologize. My heart rate increased to the point of panic. "What happened?"

"Becky really wanted to borrow your necklace . . ."

The feeling of panic turned to severe dread. She didn't even have to say which necklace. Evil-roommate-Becky only ever complimented me on one thing ever in the year I had lived with her: the diamond heart necklace my grams had given me when I graduated Boston University. The one that had belonged to my great grandma and had been given to her by my great grandfather after he graduated medical school. The diamond heart meant the world to me and now it was. . . . What? What had Evil-roommate-Becky done to my family heirloom?

"She didn't mean to, Andra. You have to know that."

"What did she do?"

Evil-Roommate-Anne actually gulped. I'd never seen an honest-to-goodness gulp before. But here Evil-Roommate-Anne was, gulping and wiping her palms on her jeans as though they were suddenly sweaty.

"She was just trying it on."

"Get it for me. Whatever she did to it, I'll fix it."

Did she gulp again?

"That's the thing. I can't get it. I was blowing my nose and then threw the tissues into the toilet. She turned to me to tell me I made disgusting noises when I blew my nose and dropped the necklace at the same time I flushed the toilet. It was accidentally flushed down." The whole sentence came out in a rush as if it was all one word.

I shook my head trying to wrap my mind around the concept of such a thing. We're those spots in my vision? "You flushed my necklace? How is that even possible? You got it back out, didn't you? Where is it now?"

Evil-Roommate-Anne began to cry. Real tears. "I called a plumber. He pulled the toilet off in case it was stuck in the little swirl shape, but it wasn't. He said the fact that it got dropped at the same time as the initial force of water was going down meant that it made it all the way to the sewers. There's no way to get it back now."

I stared at her and tried to process the pieces of information that didn't fit together no matter how hard I jammed them into the same space of my mind. "Where's Becky?"

"She's on her date." Evil-Roommate-Anne sniffled quite pathetically. I would have felt sorry for her if it hadn't been for the fact that they broke into my room to intentionally steal the only real item of sentimental value I owned.

The fact that Evil-Roommate-Becky had still gone on her date rather than face the situation directly proved her to be more evil than even I had imagined. She'd abandoned Evil-Roommate-Anne to face the music all on her own.

"It's really gone?" I had to ask. Had to know. Had to hope for one second that this was all a joke, that they really hadn't taken something so important to me and lost it forever.

She nodded.

I pressed my lips together and nodded.

Then I went to my room and pulled out my suitcases. Living here could not happen anymore. I filled the first one then texted

Emily. *Is the apartment available yet? I have got to get out of here NOW.*

She texted back almost a few minutes later. *Ummmmm about that. The original guy has moved out now and it would have been yours but something happened. The owner is choosing between you and someone else, but the other guy had some circumstances that swayed the owner in his direction. We don't know yet what exactly happened. But there apparently was some sort of fight and the apartment is now in flux. I will keep you posted.*

You don't understand Emily, I texted back. *I have to get out of this place now. If I stay another day, I might find myself killing someone. Murder does not look good on a doctor's resume.*

A long pause settled between my plea and her final response. *I will check into it.*

With nothing left to do, I hefted my two suitcases out into the hall and to the front door.

"Where are you going?" Evil-Roommate-Anne asked.

I fixed here with a glare and opened the front door instead of answering, thumping my bags over the threshold and down the stairs.

"Andra!" she called out the door. "Where are you going? What are you doing?"

I tossed my bags into the back seat of my car and went back into the house.

She followed me, repeating the questions several times. When my closet had been emptied and I'd stripped my bed of my comforter and sheets and dumped all the contents of my drawer in the kitchen into a box and hauled that to my car, she stopped asking and stopped following.

My car was packed tightly enough that I barely had room to squeeze in behind the wheel. I finally broke my silence when I felt pretty sure I'd emptied the place of my belongings. "You can keep the stuff in the fridge. You guys were just going to eat it all anyway. At least now you have my permission."

Once in my car and on the road, I had to deal with the fact that I didn't know where to go. I pulled over to the side of the road and texted Emily. *Can I have the owner's information? If I can just explain my situation, he'll know why this is so important to me.*

You know he's funny about who has his information. Let me just see what I can do, she texted back.

I wanted to tell her that I was homeless and wandering the streets on a day that had been epic when it came to bad news. But instead I texted, *Fine. Please try. This has become too toxic to bear any longer.*

I will try. Keep your chin up.

Thank you, Emily.

Her return text of, *Stay strong, Andra,* made me want to cry.

I closed my eyes and held my phone over my heart praying for a miracle that would remove me from this nightmare, opened them again, kicked the car into drive and drove until I arrived at the hospital. I parked in the parking lot, locked the car doors, and dropped my seat back as far as it would go considering all the stuff I'd crammed into the back. I allowed myself to cry a little and sleep a little and check my phone for a message from Emily a lot.

When she finally did write, it was six am.

I'm so sorry, Andra! The apartment's gone. You know this guy's reputation. He's a total misogynist prat. He always favors the guys over the girls. He found out a male med student wanted the place and gave it to him without blinking an eye. The new renter is a med student named Everett Covington. You probably know him. He's a third year, too. I guess he had some pretty major dispute with his roommate and stormed out of his old place without making a plan first. I am so sorry.

I stared at the screen in disbelief.

Everett took my apartment? My reaction felt a little shaky in the mental stability department. Everett took my apartment? I laughed. Then I gathered my toiletry case and a fresh change of clothes and entered the hospital to get ready for the day in the public restrooms.

Like a real homeless person would do.

Avoiding people proved impossible. Everett found me at just after nine am. "Hey, Andrea without an E, do you have a minute where we could talk?"

I didn't return our playful name banter. Between being tired from no sleep and feeling irrational from no humanity, I simply wasn't in the mood. I didn't even look up from taking notes on the patient I'd just visited.

"It's about Adam." He waited for a response. When he didn't receive one, he forged ahead anyway. "I just have to tell you, warn you really . . . that you shouldn't got out with him. He wouldn't be good for you."

I did turn then and the look on my face must have been at least half of what I felt because Everett actually took a step back. "You don't think he'd be good for me? Because you know so much about what's good for me? Someone has the gall to show interest in me, and you feel you have any right to act like you have a say in the situation?"

"Whoa, Andra, where is this coming from? I thought we were okay with each other, you know . . . the reset button."

I snapped my notebook closed. "I've reset the reset button." I tried to turn, to get away before tears showed up, but Everett closed his hand around my arm to stop me.

"Why? What's going on?"

My fingers instinctively went to the place where my heart necklace so often hung, but when they found nothing, anger replaced the thought of tears.

His hand that had been holding my arm moved to my shoulder where he gave it a small squeeze. The human contact wasn't enough, and it came too late.

We'd been here before. The moment reeked of déjàvu. But I couldn't stop it any more than I had been able to stop it before. "You know, it doesn't matter, Everett. You're free to date whoever you'd like, free to live wherever you'd like, free to do whatever you'd like. It's none of my business. But right now I need space . . . Literally and metaphorically. I don't have an apartment anymore, and the one I had been on the waiting list for during the last year fell through because some new student showed up and swooped it out from under me. So I have to find a place to live ASAP, and keep up with school, and I just can't do this friendship dance we keep doing."

He stared at me for several moments. "The new swooping student?" He pointed at himself. "Me?"

His shoulders dropped at my curt nod. "I see. Would it help to know why I had to move?"

I softened a little toward him. "Look, Everett, it doesn't matter. Let's just keep things professional and get through the next two years unscathed, shall we?"

His frame sagged as if his whole being cringed at the word professional. "Right. Got it. I can do that for you if that's how you really want things, but Andra, as a friend I have to warn you to keep things professional with Adam, too. He's not what you—"

"I can take care of myself."

Everett shuffled back a step, then forward a step, then he turned altogether. "I'll just leave you alone then."

When he did leave, the weight of his words pressed down on me. Alone. I felt lonelier than ever before in my life. I reached for my necklace and felt a pang. My heart was gone.

The Third
Chamber

Two people connected by the red string of fate are destined to become lovers, regardless of time, place, or circumstances.

–Chinese Legend

Chapter Eleven

Everett had been right about Adam. Adam was a lecherous kind of guy and my one and only date with him to the concert had been kind of disastrous in the had-to-call-a-cab-to keep-from-getting-date-raped kind of way. Working with them both proved difficult over the next several months. When Adam dropped school altogether because he'd been caught trifling with one of the girls in the cafeteria and because he had no hope of passing second level exams, I felt great relief to see him go.

Everett and I remained friendly toward each other but wary also, like a couple of cats who'd been in a brawl and had to still live in the same household. He dated a bit—even going so far as to actually date Tamara, though it didn't last long. He did all this while I tried not to notice. I dated less than that. I don't know if he noticed or not.

Even while we weren't dating or showing a marked interest in each other, I still sought Everett's approval. His compliments buoyed me from moment to moment. I tried to return the favor, but also had no way of knowing if my compliments meant as much to him as his did to me.

I had no way of knowing a lot of things except my job, my patients, and my relationships with the doctors and nurses, who would, hopefully, one day recommend me for residency at Boston Children's Hospital.

I kept my head down and my hands busy all through third year. Fourth year was more of the same, only with more confidence. I learned that not everyone in the hospital gave accurate information. Being proactive, asking questions—even when the wrong answers were given—and doing my own research helped me to understand the process of being a doctor. Taking the time to really learn the answers to my patient's problems allowed me to fully understand and to trust my own judgment.

At the end of our fourth year during our rotation in pediatrics, I encountered Everett sagged against the nurse's station with his head in his hands.

I slid in next to him and bumped his shoulder, a familiarity I had not allowed myself with him in all the time since I told him to keep it professional. "When was the last time you ate?" I asked as I rummaged in my pocket for what I knew he needed.

"I don't remember," Everett said.

I slipped a protein bar in his hand. "Eat this. You need it."

He lifted his head long enough to look at the package. "Honey peanut butter?"

I shrugged. "Once you eat this bar, your entire world will change. It tastes just like a honey peanut butter sandwich only it's prepackaged and doesn't smoosh and make a mess as easily. Try it."

He lifted his left eyebrow, which made me smile. I had no eyebrow control though I'd spent a great deal of time as a child staring into a mirror and trying to arch one brow. It never happened for me and was a talent I appreciated in others. "World changing?" he asked.

"World changing, rocking, domination. It's got everything."

"I can't." He pushed the bar back my direction. "It's yours."

"I've at least had lunch today, and you haven't." I totally lied. Lunch had gone the way of unicorns and Santa Claus for me . . . it just didn't happen, but I *did* keep a small supply of healthy, quick energy snacks in my pockets and had used them liberally throughout the day. I backed up and put up my hands as if to say, "No give backs."

"How about we split it?" He ripped the foil top off with his teeth, slid the bar from its packaging, and broke it exactly in half.

My stomach rumbled just then, *traitor.* I rolled my eyes and took the offered half. As if we'd planned it, we turned to each other and tapped our protein bar halves together like a toast—like we had with our red Solo cups all those years ago that felt like a different life entirely.

"Cheers," Everett said.

"Cheers."

We each took a bite, and his eyes fluttered closed briefly as if I'd just fed him ambrosia from the gods.

"Okay, this is amazing," he murmured. "It even has the texture of the honey crystallized in the bread like when my sandwich sat in my lunch bag for half the day in elementary school."

"I know! It's why I love them," I agreed.

He flipped the packaging over to see the name brand. "I am going to stock up on these."

We went to munching on our half bars in companionable silence until there was nothing left to do but get back to work. I sighed deeply as I watched Everett wad the packaging up and toss it into the waste basket.

"Sounds like a sigh with a story," Everett said.

"Not really. I just have a patient left to check in on before I can even hope to go home that I kind of dread having to look in on."

Everett eyed me with a new interest. "Did you just complain about a patient? Can I tell people about this? Not that they'd believe me or anything, but it would be great for the world to know that the great Andra Stone gets grumblers, too."

"Grumblers?" I asked.

"Patients who suck."

"Ah. I see."

"So who's your grumbler?" He lowered his voice conspiratorially, and he finally looked awake.

"We're in the pediatric wing. How can you call any kid a grumbler?"

"Nope. You don't get to pull the whole I-love-everybody card. You already admitted to dread. Kids grumble as much as anyone. So who is yours? C'mon, tell. Tell. Tell."

I laughed and swatted him lightly. "Room 204."

"The Burgess kid. Yeah, he's on my list too."

"I guess Jeremy is a bit of a grumbler . . ." I had every intention of defending the boy even as I dreaded going to his room.

"A bit?" Everett looked scandalized at the word choice. "A bit? The kid calls nurses and doctors, *this one* and *that one* and *it* as if they were inanimate objects instead of people. Any time anyone tries to talk to him about anything, his only reply is, 'Okay, yeah. I hate that.' And you want to say he's only a bit of a grumbler?"

"Well, yeah. I mean, you know . . . considering all he has going on right now. If he complains, he has a right being that his left leg is a mess. I don't mind that so much as he's just . . ."

"A grumbler . . ." Everett prodded. He literally prodded. He poked my shoulder several times as if he was one of the very grumbly kids he was just complaining about.

"No. It isn't his grumbling that makes me dread going to his room. It's just that . . . well, honestly? He stinks."

"Isn't that what we're talking about?"

"Not that he stinks as in he's lame, but stinks as in he smells bad. Really bad."

Everett laughed out loud. "Stinks? All that kid has wrong with him on a societal level, and you're worried about his smell? I haven't really spent any time in his room. Is it like bodily fluids? Is our resident grumbler a bed wetter too?"

"It's not that," I said. "He's on a catheter since he can't walk on that leg, not that I'm afraid of a little urine. But what he smells like is so much worse." I shook my head and tried to find the right words to explain myself. "The kid smells like . . . like hot dog water."

If Everett had thought a stinky kid was funny before, he thought hot dog water was absolutely hilarious.

"You must be tired," I said, "because none of this is really funny. How long have you been here today?"

"You just compared a child to hot dog water. It's totally funny. And I got here at the same time you did." He shot me a knowing look with the eyebrow raised again.

His bringing up the reality of our very long day made me rub at my eyes. I tried to do so without looking like I felt the tired seeping into my veins and being systematically pumped through my body, but Everett watched me closely. Of course he noticed.

"You work too hard, Andrea without an E."

I looked at him, *really* looked at him for the first time in months. How did I suddenly miss him so badly when we'd been working together in such close proximity for such a long time? "You work too hard, too." The words came out slowly, softly. "Maybe we both need some time to unwind. We could go get a pizza—"

"I *do* take time to unwind," he said, avoiding the fact that I'd made the first overture to something more—an opportunity to spend time together that I thought he'd jump at after being placed firmly at arm's length for so long.

Instead, he almost seemed to jump away. And then, as if someone had ordered her from a menu with instantaneous delivery service, from around the corner, a woman appeared—a woman I recognized from around the hospital but hadn't given any thought to how she fit in or why she loitered in our area every once in a while.

"Evs!" she called out. "You ready?"

Did everyone call Everett *Evs* but me? The nickname stabbed my sensibilities like toothpicks under my fingernails.

Everett smiled at me. The smile seemed sad, and it made me feel a little sad to see it. "You do need to unwind, Andra. You're going to implode if you don't. No one can keep up that kind of pace."

And with that, his arm slid around the woman's waist. He said, "You've met Liz, haven't you?"

I sucked in a deep breath. "No, I haven't." Was my smile tight? Too forced? Was I even smiling at all? Deciding it would be wrong to reach up my hand to feel at my cheeks to see if I was smiling, I extended it to this interloper instead. "Hello, Liz. I'm Andra. It's nice to meet you."

She shook my hand and smiled back like she was happy to meet me. "I know. Evs is always talking about the med student who sometimes knows more than the doctors. It's nice to finally get an introduction beyond just seeing you around when I've stopped by to help keep this one fed." She put her hand on his stomach and gave it a little pat.

Everett gave her a squeeze as he nodded in my direction. "Andra beat you to the punch today. She shared a peanut butter and honey sandwich with me."

Liz shot me a grateful glance. "Thanks for watching out for him. I always thought doctors were smart about health, but it turns out they're only smart about other people's health and totally oblivious to their own."

"The struggle is real," I commented, not even sure what I meant to be saying. I didn't like Everett's arm around her. I didn't like how casually she accepted that he belonged to her.

I didn't like that his moving on was good for him.

I loathed that his moving on was all my fault.

Liz focused on Everett with such admiration, it would have been adorable if she'd been looking at anyone else. "Well, babe, any chance they'll let you off soon? I downloaded a movie—one you'll love."

I was curious if she had any idea what kind of movies Everett actually liked. Did she know he was a sucker for science fiction? Did she know he practically had all the Dr. Who episodes memorized? Was she aware that he cried in the ending to the fourth episode of Star Wars because he loved it so much and cried in the third episode because he thought it was so lame?

Did she know my Everett like I knew my Everett?

"What movie?" He asked the question I itched to ask.

"Old classic. You told me it was one of your favorites. *Fifth Element.*"

My heart felt like it fell out of my chest and flopped around on the floor. She did know.

"And I ordered Thai for dinner. No stress tonight. Just relax."

The look of gratitude he gave her pinged my chest.

"I think I can leave. I'll check and make sure, then we can go," he told her while swinging her in the direction they would need to walk to find out. "You going to be okay, Andrea without an E?" He tossed me a look over his shoulder.

I raised my clipboard into the air. "I've got hot dog water waiting for me. I couldn't possibly be better." I laughed, because laughing made it hurt a little less.

Liz looked over her shoulder too. "That doesn't sound fun at all. You look like you can use a break too. We have enough food. Want to join us for dinner and a movie?"

Did she need to be nice on top of everything?

"No, thanks. I've got dinner plans." *With my microwave,* I added silently. Everett must have seen the truth of it because his stupid eyebrow arched for a third time. It no longer seemed cute to me. And how had we been friends all these years and I never knew he could do that? Did he acquire the talent to impress Liz? Was it new? Or was I just oblivious?

I squared my shoulders. My choices belonged to me, and decisions were made to be lived with, as my grams always said. I chose to keep things professional between Everett and me.

Regretting such decisions just because I felt a little tired and weak didn't help anyone. With my clipboard clutched to my chest, there remained nothing left to do but face the boy who smelled like hot dog water.

"Have fun, guys," I said and headed down the hall.

"You should go home, too, Andra. You need a break," he called after me, but I waved him away with a laugh and a noncommittal grunt.

As my feet made soft thuds on the hall floor, Everett's words struck a chord that thrummed a little. I did need a break. So instead of visiting the boy that smelled like hot dog water and had a little attitude to match, I stopped by to check on Drake, a little boy who had been badly burned over half his face, his shoulder, and down his back by a pan of boiling water.

The burns would leave irreparable scars on a face that would have otherwise been very handsome when he grew up.

He was a dear little guy who was pretty much terrified of the entire hospital staff. But he wasn't afraid of me. And just like I calmed him down, he also calmed me. We were good for each other that way. Who needed boyfriend companionship when sweet little boy companionship was more than enough?

Before I'd even moved both feet into the room with Drake, I focused on my very best friendly-doctor voice and asked out loud, "And how's my favorite patient doing?" When someone else looked up from Drake's chart and smiled at me, my feet stuttered to a stop.

"Hello?" I said, the tone of those two words could have been translated any number of ways: Who the heck are you? Why are you in my patient's room looking at my patient's chart? And why am I suddenly very nervous?

95

Staring at the woman made me feel like I had an oral presentation to give that I hadn't prepared for.

I tossed a glance to little Drake in the bed. He slept, oblivious to the newcomer in his room. Still waiting for an answer from the woman, I turned my attention back to her.

"You must be the Andra Stone I've heard so much about," the woman said. She was shorter than me, which was saying something since I was considered a hobbit in most circles. But she wasn't a lot shorter than me—a couple inches at most.

She looked to be Chinese, but her accent was so mild and unobtrusive that if I hadn't really been paying attention to her, I might not have noticed it at all. At first glance, she appeared to be about fifty years old, but then she almost seemed to shift, even with my eyes trained on her. She might have been forty. Her black hair was done up in a messy bun at the back of her head and she seemed genuinely happy to see me, which was a little disconcerting.

"Yes. I'm Andra Stone," I said. When she merely blinked at me with a vague sort of smile that made me feel like she knew something I didn't know, I prodded her to speak again. "And you are?"

The woman lowered the chart. "You may call me Miss Pearl."

I narrowed my eyes as if I could tunnel my vision enough to see her better. "Miss Pearl?" I knew the name and searched back through my memory for why. "You're the one who recommended that Everett transfer schools."

She took a deep gratified breath. "Ah, dear Everett. He is a lovely young man." She tilted her head and strode closer to me until she had pressed up against, but not actually entered, my personal space bubble. "Don't you think?"

I sidestepped her and held out my hand, indicating she should give up the chart in her hands. Miss Pearl was an actual doctor and she now worked administration, which all meant that acting impertinent could be bad for me, but the woman unsettled my nerves, which made me need to be doing something. The only thing I knew how to do was check on the patient.

Miss Pearl gave up the chart without complaint or question. She handed it off to me as if I was the greater authority regarding the medical care of little Drake Armstrong. As an actual doctor, she clearly had seniority. Her letting me take over felt like a test.

She watched me work, her scrutiny suffocating. I tugged at the collar of my shirt several times, even though it was loose.

Needing to break the silence, I asked, "So what brings you to UMASS? Are you working in our department now?"

Miss Pearl smiled, amused at something she didn't seem likely to share with me. "Yes. I am working in *your* department, now. I started working in Everett's department first, but well . . . that didn't turn out like planned. The boy has given up entirely."

She must have meant when she worked at Tufts before Everett transferred to UMASS. But Everett hadn't given up. He was a great student. He would graduate with the ability to do his internship anywhere he wanted. He was just that good. Besides, it had seemed that his leaving had been all her idea.

Little Drake woke up and half-smiled at me from a face half-covered in bandages. His dark hair stuck out in fifty different crazy angles. He winced as he tried to sit up, likely from the pain of his dressings causing friction against his burned shoulder and back. I helped him up. "You okay, buddy?" I asked.

He nodded and then noticed the other person in the room. "Who's that?" he asked.

"That's Doctor Pearl," I said.

Miss Pearl came close to his bed and took his hand in hers. "Just call me Miss Pearl, dear."

He didn't mind Doctor Miss Pearl touching him, which was nice because he didn't let many people touch him. I was one of the few on the allowed list. Most of the nurses and other med students made him howl when they went too near, which made changing the dressings on his wounds a difficult task.

Her eyes softened as she held his hand. "I see into your heart, little one. You're worried you look like a monster," she told the child.

I gasped at the horror of such a naked truth, but she cast me a stern glance that shut me up.

"But I promise you that you are still quite handsome, and in a few years, when you're old enough to know real love, you will meet me again, and I will help you find a girl who will see you for the beautiful young man you are." She leaned down so they were eye level. "Trust me, Drake. Trust a woman who knows everything about such matters. When things get dark, and you find yourself worrying, you remember that Miss Pearl has excellent plans for you."

His big eyes had latched onto her as if she might be the only thing holding him upright. He nodded. "I trust you, Miss Pearl."

She patted his hand. "Good boy," she said. She finally returned her attention to me. "But now we need to help this young woman to trust me."

I narrowed my eyes at her. "I don't have any reason not to," I said even while thinking, *although this total weirdness with my patient is freaking me out and you used the word monster to a little boy who is having major self-image drama.*

Miss Pearl gave another of her knowing smiles, almost like she'd heard what I'd thought. The very idea made me blush and feel out of sorts.

"Are you okay, Doc Stone?" Drake asked. He insisted on calling me Doc even though I hadn't graduated yet.

"I'm fine, buddy. Just fine." A quick glance up to see that Miss Pearl eyed me like a toad might eye a fly made me feel far less than fine.

I finished with Drake and took a deep breath—sucking in oxygen as if it was determination—and headed to the room of Jeremy Burgess. Miss Pearl fell into step beside me.

Great.

As if she didn't make me nervous enough while attending to a nice kid, having her witness the inner workings of hot-dog-water boy practically paralyzed me.

"What is *that*?" Jeremy asked as soon as Miss Pearl and I stepped into his room. The hot dog water aroma slammed me and made me want to vomit. What oozed from that kid's pores?

"We do not refer to other humans as *that*," I told him for the millionth time. "*She* is someone you need to respect." With his helicopter crazy mom not in the room, lecturing the hot dog water boy liberated me from all the times I hadn't said anything because I worried what his mom would say about it.

"What does *it* do?" he asked, steamrolling right over the top of my lecture.

"*SHE* is a doctor." I wanted to add that if he made her mad, she'd take out his spleen while he slept, but even with his mom gone, Miss Pearl still observed as a witness. I'd never get away with it.

"I hate doctors," he said with a petulance that only someone who lived his whole life with a sullen, sour disposition could manage.

Miss Pearl stabbed a fierce glare in the child's direction. The intensity was enough that if Jeremy's leg hadn't been mangled, he'd have made a break for it and likely never stopped running. "I have not been referred to as an inanimate object for many, many, many years—more years than you can even imagine. I remember a time when uncles and men in our village would say to my parents that the stones in the garden were worth more than a daughter. They would tsk at my parents and say that a girl was like lice in the rice. I remember the shame of such words, but it has been a long time since anyone spoke with such vinegar on their tongues to me. And I am no longer the girl who will tolerate such treatment. You will apologize." She folded her arms and stared him down.

I glanced at the door, wondering when the helicopter mom would return and whether or not she would file a complaint against the hospital for the staff strong-arming her kid into some sort of humanity.

The doorway remained empty.

When I looked back to Jeremy, I found that he had also been staring at the door, probably wondering where his mom was as well.

"I don't have to apologize," Jeremy finally said, straightening himself in his bed to make himself look as tall and as important as possible.

Miss Pearl considered for a long time before she answered. I shot another glance at the door, waiting for the moment when his mom exploded into the middle of our power struggle.

"You're right," Miss Pearl said finally.

I frowned. "What?"

Jeremy frowned too. "Come again?"

"You do not have to apologize. But I promise a boy who does not apologize for anything, finds himself with much debt in his heart. That debt is heavy and unattractive. Do you know what I am, boy?" She leaned in close. I almost gagged to see her lean in so close, knowing what kind of odors that kid could waft into the air with just a movement of his arm.

He shook his head slowly.

"I am the one who repairs hearts. I am the one who fills in the cracks and sews up the jagged tears of life. Do you really want to come to a day when you need your heart mended and find me unwilling to do that service for you because I cannot in good conscience allow you to go into further debt when I know you have no means of repayment? Do you really want to gamble on whether or not I will have mercy and do you the service for free?"

I swear five whole minutes passed without either of them speaking or blinking. The questions she asked hung in the air between them.

"I . . . I'm sorry," Jeremy said.

I moved back in case lightning decided to strike to celebrate the moment. The Burgess kid said sorry. Wonders never ceased.

Miss Pearl worked a miracle in the hospital. She might not have directly saved the kid's life, but I was willing to bet she indirectly saved it. If he could manage an apology every now and again, it might save him from being strangled in his future.

And wow! Miss Pearl knew how to put the theatrics on what we did. She made being a heart surgeon sound like a superpower. I wanted to remember how she phrased it: fills in the cracks and sews up the jagged tears of life . . . beautiful.

But Miss Pearl wasn't quite through with Jeremy. "You would do well to remember that no woman worthy of having would ever align herself with a man who does not respect other humans. Calling a person *this* or *that* or *it* not only robs them of their humanity, it robs you of yours."

"Yes, ma'am," Jeremy said, his eyes wide with wonder at his own words.

The boy who smelled like hot dog water had agreed with another person.

"And this talk," Miss Pearl went on, "of you hating doctors is absurd. Who do you think is fixing your leg? Who do you think is making it so you can walk without being lame and run without a shamble? It is the men and women who are caring for you. You do not say that you hate them when they've done no ill to you. Gratitude is one of the finest qualities in a person. If you can manage to show some gratitude to your doctors and then to any other person who does you a kindness, there might come a time when you see me again in your life, and I will give you a kindness unlike any you could ever imagine. But it must be earned, and I will know if it is not."

Jeremy nodded and finally looked away from her and fixed his attention on me. To have him look at me directly with such an abashed expression on his face startled me.

"I'm sorry," he told me.

I about needed a doctor myself because the kid nearly gave me a heart attack.

Not too long after that, Jeremy's mother returned to his bedside. "I had your teachers bring me your schoolwork so you could do it while you sit here, if you feel like it. You don't have to." She hurried to add on that last bit before he could give his typical snarky retort of how much he hated school and hated homework and would rather eat slugs than do something so tedious and absurd. "I want you to focus on getting better. If not doing your work helps, then that's fine with me." She gave him a fretful smile and a loving pat on his hand.

His gaze slid to Miss Pearl and then back to his mother, who hovered over him with more skill than the most practiced helicopter pilot. "Thanks, Mom. This will help me not get behind."

Miss Pearl beamed at him. I was pretty sure my bottom jaw hit the floor. His mother gasped and asked him if he was feeling all right. She even double checked with me to see if he had a fever of some sort. Even more amazing, the smell had shifted, and not just because I'd grown used to it, but because the room actually smelled different.

It smelled like a lotion Janette used to have in our apartment all those years ago—a lotion with cherry blossoms. It smelled like Drake's room had when I'd first entered. Miss Pearl must wear the same kind of lotion as Janette used to.

"So what are you?" I asked Miss Pearl as we walked toward the nurse's station "The child whisperer?"

She laughed. "No, I merely have a talent for seeing people in all the ways they are."

"People are more than one way?" I moved to keep from getting run over by Janice, a nurse who was excessively efficient and speedy at her job and didn't have a problem mowing people over if they were in her way when she had a task to do.

"Of course they are," Miss Pearl said. "A person has as much variety to them as a field of wild flowers. They have pasts and presents and futures. They are part of the past, they are the person that is in the present and they have a million and two options for who they can be in the future based on the past and the present. I see the options they have, the paths in front of them."

"You see the future?" I was starting to wonder if Miss Pearl needed a visit to the psyche ward.

"I see possibility. I am a pretty good guess at the sort of paths a person wants to take. Sometimes the real struggle is convincing them to take it." She narrowed her eyes at me and smiled as if some deeper meaning hid under her words and she expected me to understand what the meaning might be. It had been too long since I'd had a decent night's sleep. As it was, I felt like I'd just witnessed some sort of voodoo in Jeremy Burgess's room.

"Huh," was the only reply I could think to give.

"Hmph," was her reply.

She fell silent, which worried me that somehow I'd offended her. I tried at a different conversation. "So you're a heart doctor, right? That's your specialty, isn't it?" I asked.

"Yes," she said. "Matters of the heart are my specialty."

"Are you here permanently, Doc—" I caught myself before realizing she'd never given a last name. "Doctor Pearl?"

Was it Doctor Pearl? Was Pearl her last name or her first? How was I to know when she kept telling everyone to call her Miss Pearl?

We finally arrived at the nurses' station, but no one manned it. Strange. Usually someone sat watch over the station at all times. I pulled out my notebook and used the counter to jot some quick notes about both the boys I'd visited, but I felt Pearl's gaze sear a hole through the side of my head.

"I will be here as long as I need to be." She'd waited so long to answer my question, I almost forgot I asked one. "My purpose is to check on the behavior of a few staff members and the way they handled my student when I transferred him to this location. He's a bright boy with much to offer. I don't feel he has been treated as well as he deserves."

She had to mean Everett. But how could she say he wasn't being treated well? All the staff loved him and were more loyal to him than they were to half of the actual staff. Everett enriched the working environment for everyone. He built others up, he kept up on his own studies so he always had a correct and smart answer. I half felt like telling Miss Pearl that she could go home because Everett had found success without her help, and he would likely be mortified if he knew she was here drumming up favors for him.

I put down my pen and notebook so I could face her square on. "Everett is totally capable. You do know that, right? He doesn't need special treatment. He's smart and is great with the patients. Everyone loves him."

"I see. Everyone loves him. But do you love him, Andra Stone?"

I shot a panicked look to the station, which was empty, and to the halls, which were also empty and wondered where everyone had disappeared to, all while being incredibly grateful they were gone. Relief flooded me at the same time confusion slammed into me. No one heard the question. No rumors could come from this moment.

But the question itself caused the confusion. It stirred up memories of Everett smiling at me, of the way it felt when he kissed me all those years ago; it made me wish he stood in front of me right that moment so I could kiss him again.

"Of course I do," I said, then shook myself, wondering why I had said such a thing. "I mean I don't. I mean I do care about him a great deal. I care about everyone here."

Miss Pearl watched me sputter for an answer and then said, "It must be a terribly strange thing to want to be a heart surgeon."

This statement confused me more than anything. I straightened hard as if pressed flat against a wall. Who was she to say such a thing? Did she view me as Everett's competition? "It's all I ever wanted to be, and I'm good at it."

"Yet you know so little of your own heart."

"There you are!" Graham, one of the other students, exclaimed from down the hall. "Dr. Lentz has been looking for you!"

I pointed in Miss Pearl's direction with the intention of using the new admin as my alibi, but she no longer stood next to the counter with me. I looked to my other side and then did a circle to see if she'd sneaked around behind me, but no, she wasn't anywhere.

"Well?" Graham said. "Are you coming?"

"Right away," I murmured and hurried to follow him, even while I searched the halls for any sign of the mysterious Chinese doctor who asked impossible questions and said terrible things.

But she'd gone.

I shook my head hard and glanced behind me again. Had I imagined her? Part of me hoped I really had just imagined the formidable woman, because the one question she asked bothered me more than anything anyone had ever said to me.

Do you love him?

But if I had imagined it, why would my imagination want me to answer a question that made me so acutely uncomfortable?

Chapter Twelve

Nope. I hadn't imagined Miss Pearl. She seemed like my personal shadow. I never saw her bothering any of the other students, but she trailed after me as if someone had stitched her to my heels.

She chattered nonstop about Everett. She listed his qualities to me backwards and forwards as if she planned on giving an exam later and wanted me to get an A. But she was never around when Everett and I came anywhere near each other. She just vanished, as I'd come to find she had a way of doing. If she hadn't been my superior, I would have asked her to haunt someone else for a while, but since she arrived at UMASS with the intention of surveying the staff and probably reporting back on her findings, I remained positive and helpful and resigned to the fact that she had made me her go-to girl.

When I brought her up to the other students, they raised their eyebrows at me in a way that made me feel stupid. They were right. Complaining about a superior ran a med student aground faster than anything else. Even a crummy student who remained positive was likely to get better placement for residency than a brilliant student with a craptastic attitude.

But I really wanted to complain, and not just about Miss Pearl, but about Everett's girlfriend Liz, too. Liz hung out more and more at the hospital.

Couldn't she wait in the car instead of in my territory?

Her continual loitering led me to feel great surprise to find Everett alone in the hall, leaning up against a wall and looking down at his phone.

A quick check around us proved that he really was alone . . . except for me.

"Everest without an S," I said.

He looked up from his phone. "Andrea without an E."

He looked so tired that all my sympathies pinged with understanding. I was so tired too. So I slumped against the wall next to him and looked down at his phone. "Candy Crush?"

He laughed. "Nope. More like soul crush."

I straightened. "What happened?"

"My sister's business is opening a new location this weekend. My mom demands that I be there."

"Don't you want to go support your sister?"

He laughed again; only this time the sound that came out dripped with acrimony. "I might if it was left up to me to make my own choice. But our mother shoving me feels . . ." he scratched at the back of his neck in agitation. "Feels like shoving."

"I'm sorry. I know what family obligations are like."

"You're one of the few who do. Most people think I'm just being a jerk, but they don't get it. You have to live with my family to really get it." He sighed. "It would be better if I didn't have to go alone."

It shouldn't have made me brighten. It really shouldn't have. But it did. "No Liz?"

He shook his head and glanced down the hall at a couple of orderlies laughing about something we probably didn't want to know about. "She has obligations this weekend." He looked like he might have been about to say more when his eyes fell on me, and he stopped.

I glanced back to the orderlies who were already past and then back to where he stared at me as if he hadn't ever seen me before. "What?"

"Will you do me a favor? A huge one? One for which I will owe you for the rest of my life?"

"Depends. I refuse to put a hit out on your sister, or your mother for that matter." I didn't promise not to put one on Liz.

"You won't have to. I just need you to come with me this weekend."

I did not see that one coming. I was pretty sure he meant out of town. "Isn't your sister in Maine?"

"Yes. Which is why I need a buddy. I'll have to stay at my parents' place, and I am not going to that house alone."

Everett was inviting me away for the weekend? It must have been because I was tired. Or maybe it was because Miss Pearl had followed me around for days telling me about all things Everett. Because I shrugged and the words, "Sure. Why not?" fell out of my mouth.

He pushed off from the wall and wrapped his arms around me, his relief a tangible thing. "Thank you, Andra. Thank you for not making me go this alone."

I laughed. "You've held my hand through my family parties before. I can return the favor."

He squeezed a little tighter and my eyes fluttered closed briefly, enjoying the nearness of him. How long had it been since I'd had human contact of this sort? Too long. Too long since I'd felt the comfort of someone's touch. Such contact was pivotal in humans. I'd read the studies where babies died in an orphanage after their nurses were only allowed to cuddle half the children. They were told to leave the other half alone and care only for their basic needs of feeding and cleaning, instead. The half not given human contact died rather than soldier on to face a world alone.

Had I allowed myself to become one of those babies in some sort of self-exile from human touch?

Yes.

Now that someone's arms held me securely in that exchange of energy that made being human worth it, I realized how much the contact meant to me, how absent it had been from my life, how desperate I was for Everett to never let go.

But he did let go.

We were in the hallway where anyone might come upon us and see. We were supposed to be working, not fraternizing.

When he released me, we shared an awkward smile and I took a shaky step away from him—just to prove I had the strength to move away. Proving it to him or proving it to myself, either way it was proof.

"I'll pick you up Friday evening at six. Is that okay? We could probably stretch it a little later, but we really need to be on the road by six-thirty if we want to arrive at any decent kind of hour."

"Sounds great. I'll pack before leaving for the hospital in the morning just to make sure I'm ready."

"Fabulous." His eyes captured mine, almost reeling me in and pulling me back that step I'd used to distance us. "Seriously, thanks, Andra. You've always been a good friend to me."

I nodded, not trusting myself to answer the strangeness of my feelings. He tapped my shoulder and returned to work, leaving me there in the hall and nearly toppling over from leaning into his energy that was no longer right in front of me.

"You still love him."

I jumped at the voice that came from behind me and placed my hand over my heart to try to hold it from leaping out of my chest. "Miss Pearl! You scared me."

She grinned, knowing perfectly well she'd nearly stopped my heart by sneaking up on me like that. As a heart doctor, she should have known better than to do such things. But then . . . maybe as a heart doctor, she knew she could get it running again if she accidentally stopped the thing.

Recovering from the shock of her presence nearly made me forget what she'd said. Before I could form any sort of response, she'd breezed off down the hall in the same direction Everett had gone.

My heart went from stopped to pounding wildly. Would she tell Everett that I still had feelings for him? I followed her before I even knew what I was doing. Everett had a girlfriend, a nice girlfriend. I couldn't have Miss Pearl announcing my emotional status to him as though we were both in grade school.

When I turned the same corner, she'd disappeared again. Everett was there and flashed me a questioning look before turning back to the little girl in the wheelchair. After a thorough check of my surroundings, the only logical conclusion was that Miss Pearl had taken the stairs to a different floor. She wasn't anywhere to be seen on this one.

Trying not to feel stupid—first for being so transparent to Everett and second for being so transparent to Miss Pearl, I returned to my work, thinking only one thing: that Pearl woman must have rocked hide and seek as a kid.

Chapter Thirteen

Several days later, Everett picked me up at my apartment right at six. He didn't comment on my apartment at all, and part of me wondered if we were thinking the same thing about living arrangements and his living in the apartment I'd wanted.

Things worked out okay for me in spite of everything, so I no longer had reason to complain, but imagining his position in the apartment I'd wanted made me smile a little and shake my head.

Would we have come to a different place if I hadn't been so mad about that situation?

Maybe.

My smile faded with the thoughts of what might have happened and the fact that they didn't happen.

"You okay?" Everett asked.

I forced the smile back. "Great. Why?"

"You looked like someone kicked your puppy just now."

I laughed. That was certainly one way to put it. "Really, I'm fine."

He loaded my bags into the back of his black truck and we were off. Once on the freeway headed in the general direction of Maine, I ran my hands over the leather seat. "So, I don't remember you being a truck guy. When did this happen?"

He ducked his head into a sorta shrug. "I know what you're thinking. You're comparing me to Greg right now, aren't you? But it isn't like that. The old car broke down and while I was out looking for options, Liz mentioned how much she loved trucks and one thing led to another and the next thing I knew, I was driving this off the lot."

It took me a moment to know what to say in response. Liz had made a suggestion that he followed up on. My skin numbed at the thought, forcing a shiver from me. Which made me feel incredibly disingenuous. I'd brushed him off all those years ago, and then brushed him off again more recently. Any kind of decent human would rejoice that he had found happiness. Instead, I wanted to hunker down with a movie and a box of raspberry filled donuts.

I shivered again.

"Are you cold?" He adjusted the temperature in the cab until warm air flowed. Since explaining that the climate had nothing to do with the current numb feeling I had was out of the question, I went on to other topics, safer topics, topics that could have nothing to do with Liz.

I talked about medicine. We discussed our preferences for residencies, our most complicated patients, nurses we loved, nurses we loathed, which doctors made us cringe with their incompetence, and which made us want to applaud for their brilliance.

We talked about treatments and internal medicine, diseases and symptoms. Never before had any conversation stimulated my intellect more. We were so compatible in our field, so like-minded, and so similar in our skill that I wondered how I had ever walked away from him. Where else would I find a man who provided riveting, thoughtful, sensitive conversation?

I shoved away all internal debate as to whether or not I only felt this way because Miss Pearl had been pressing the topic of Everett with such tenacity. Did it matter why I allowed myself to entertain thoughts that had been stifled for so long? Wasn't it better to explore possibilities while they were still in front of me?

I snuggled down into the leather seat of the truck Liz picked out and allowed myself to consider.

The five hour ride to Maine flew by too quickly. It felt like we'd only begun conversing and then we were done. His headlights briefly flashing on an older but obviously expensive home before he cut his engine, and the headlights along with it. We opened doors, stepped into the dark, and unloaded our luggage.

The smell of the air reminded me a great deal of living in Boston, where the ocean bumped into the city and the smells of both battled for dominance. Clearly, wherever we were, the ocean wasn't too far away.

Everett smiled at me. "Are you ready for this?"

"Bring it."

We both squared our shoulders to approach the front door.

Everett often compared his family to mine, which was more than enough reason to make me feel apprehensive, but even more was the idea of meeting the parents. Meet-the-parents experiences in my past were few and far between. Most relationships never made enough headway to merit getting the family involved.

Not that Everett and I were in a relationship. But meeting Everett's parents filled me with an anxiety to please that had never existed before. I wanted this impression to be an excellent one.

"Here goes nothing." Everett pressed the doorbell button, sending a cascade of distant chimes through the rooms inside, and we waited.

I wanted to ask why he had to ring the bell instead of just walk in. These people were his parents, weren't they? This was his family home, wasn't it? Didn't kids have some kind of natural right to gain entry to the home of their childhood without the formality of the doorbell? Maybe my family was more chill than I ever gave them credit for.

Before long, a shadow passed over the faceted crystal sidelight, and the door swung open. "I wondered what was taking you so long!" The tall, thin woman ushered us into the house with these words as if we'd been caught doing something wrong and she wanted us to now come in while she called the authorities. Everett made an *after you* motion with his hands, so I followed the woman into the front foyer. Everett came along behind me and closed the door, eliminating our one shot at escape.

The woman inspected us, or actually inspected *me*.

I inspected her right back. Her dark, not-quite-shoulder-length haircut that a lot of women wore in middle age, didn't make her resemble a typical mom, like it did most of the women who wore it. Instead it gave a natural texture to her entire person. She smiled with lips that were as naked as they were on the day she'd been born, making me rub my own glossy lips together. I didn't wear much makeup, but next to Everett's mom, I felt like the painted lady. His mom was actually very pretty and didn't need the enhancement of mascara and lip color, but still . . .

Even if I looked okay without mascara, which I didn't, I never wanted to give up lip gloss. Dried out lips that stuck together when you tried to open your mouth were not only icky to look at for other people, but they felt gross. I smiled with my glossy lips and felt no shame in them. Everyone had their own path to take. I put out my hand to meet this woman who stared at me with eyes so blue, they looked like they'd been chipped from glacial ice. I briefly wondered where Everett's brown, gold, green eyes came from as she took my hand and said, "You must be the girl Everett told his sister about. What is it you do?"

"I'm a medical student with Everett." I sketched a glance at Everett. Did his mom think she was talking to Liz?

He shifted uncomfortably.

"Well, I think that's just wonderful!" she said. "Medicine is a fabulous profession and perfect for women who can be compassionate and competent at the same time. I've always wondered how that particular career path became the stereotypical man's job."

"And it starts," Everett muttered from behind me. "Hello, Grace," he said, only this time loudly enough to be heard by both of us.

I shot a look over my shoulder and then back to his mom. My confusion seemed to amuse her.

"I taught my children to call me by my name a long time ago. I think titles like *mom* or *mother* pigeonhole women into roles they don't always belong in." She smiled wide through her naked lips.

Was I supposed to be amused at that also, or horrified?

I felt a little of both. He'd warned me she was unlike any kind of feminist I'd met before. How right he had been. I was absolutely for equal rights for everybody, but I also absolutely wanted to own the title of *mom* when I decided to have children. If my kids called me Andra, I would have felt like I'd deprived them, and me, of something kind of fabulous. Plus, it would've ticked me off, and I'd likely ground them for being disrespectful. Just like I expected people to call me doctor when I graduated med school, I expected a particular little person to call me mom when I graduated pregnancy. The title was earned.

But to each her own.

Grace began moving to the stairs at the right of the entryway. "Your rooms are ready. I was actually kind of surprised Everett didn't book you both a hotel but then . . . well, it figures, doesn't it?"

Everett huffed behind me, and I felt like my neck would break with all the looking behind me to him and in front of me to her.

Was she insulting her son for real? And in front of me? Who did that? Even my father, who hated my going to medical school and hated that my brother was in culinary school, never talked either one of us down in front of other people. His sense of place and propriety and staying in society's good standing didn't allow him the freedom to say whatever he really thought of his disappointing children where anyone could hear. Doing so would reflect badly on him.

Not certain she meant the hotel comment as an insult, and trying to make sure her and I were clear on whose side I was on, I said, "Being that we're both in medical school and working to be responsible with our finances so we don't leave with a debt load we can't recover from, booking a hotel would have been a really foolish move when your hospitality is obviously so open to us."

I lied, of course. At that moment I really wish Everett had booked a hotel. I would have been willing to put it on my credit card. And it wasn't that she'd said much wrong exactly, but more that she felt *off* enough to not be exactly hospitable. My parents had never greeted me in such a chairman-of-the-board way. It felt unnatural. And it wasn't that she didn't hug him. Lots of families weren't touchy-feely like that, but she didn't really acknowledge him either. She saw me, spoke to me. She spoke around him and about him, but not to him. When he'd said hello to her, she hadn't even returned the greeting.

She stopped half way up the stairs and looked back at me. "Oh yes, of course!" she said finally as if she'd analyzed my words and decided they were pro her. "My home is always open to helping out young women while they're in their formative educational years. I wouldn't dream of having you stay anywhere else."

Her prior comment made it sounded like she more than dreamed of us staying elsewhere, but oh well.

"Is Riley staying in a hotel?" Everett asked.

"Of course not." She acted surprised he would ask such a thing. He made a soft snort.

Riley also lived out of state, though her Rhode Island was definitely closer than Massachusetts. I shifted my bag to my other shoulder as we made it to the top of the stairs so I didn't bump it against the wall of pictures in the hall.

And there were a lot of pictures.

There was a family photo of everyone, the final high school picture from each of the three children, one professional more current photo from each of the children and each of the adults, and there were a couple dozen other photos of the two daughters in varying activities.

There was only the two of Everett—three if you counted the family photo.

There were pictures of the girls in caps and gowns, pictures of one in what looked like a medical clinic, surrounded by children; and that same girl at the top of Machu Picchu; pictures of another in a business suit standing in front of law offices; pictures of marathon races and the girls holding awards.

I glanced back at Everett, but he only smiled and shrugged.

She showed me to my room first and that was where they left me. Everett said, "I'll drop off my bag and come back to check on you to make sure you have everything you need."

Grace bristled a little at this, though I couldn't see why, but then the door was closed, and I plopped onto the bed and sighed in great relief.

The tension between those two was thicker than concrete.

No wonder Everett wanted an accomplice on this trip. No wonder he acted as though I'd thrown him a lifeline when I agreed to go.

"And I thought my mother was crazy," I said aloud to the room made up to be very French provincial. The satin covered headboard and cream satin bedspread over a frilly lace cream bed skirt, along with the chandelier with sparkling little crystals dangling from the lights meant to look like candles, were an obvious style choice.

Grace didn't strike me as the sort of woman who would stylize her house so traditionally. I expected more of a minimalist style, with big red square cushions and a single blanket over them, making up the bed; with maybe a boxy square desk and a boxy square chair, which just went to show that people cannot be second guessed.

Everett was back in just a moment. He knocked lightly.

"Come in," I said.

He did, and, gratefully, he entered the room alone.

"Where's your mom?" I asked.

He shrugged. That would, apparently, be all the answer I could expect for that question because he then asked. "Are you exhausted or would you be interested in going for a short walk before we tuck in for the night?"

Oddly, even after a full day at the hospital, a five hour drive, and a grueling five minutes with his mother, I was anything but tired. "A walk sounds great."

We vacated our rooms and took a set of back stairs that led to the kitchen and out a back door. From there, the moonlight reflected a bright silver swath over the water, greeting us with a view of the ocean.

"This is your backyard?" Did my voice sound jealous? Because I certainly felt jealous.

He shoved his hands in his pockets and grinned at it, obviously very pleased with his backyard. "It's the only real perk to enduring my family, but it's always worth it."

He guided me around patio furniture and to a stone path. In an obvious attempt to avoid the topic of his mother, he asked, "I heard Dr. Jensen let you do the stitching during the surgery rotation."

"Who told you that?" I asked, laughing.

"Dr. Niles when we met up in the cafeteria. We were talking about the specialty fields our classmates would be going into. When I told him I wanted to be a heart surgeon, he mentioned how Dr. Jensen actually let you do the stitching, which we all know is unheard of because Dr. Jensen never lets med students do anything but watch his amazing expertise. "

"He's not that bad," I countered, feeling a blush of pride from knowing that Dr. Jensen *was* that bad. The guy never let med students do anything, and if they stood too close, he'd glare at them until they backed up a step or two. He did not want them in his space, interfering with his business. He was a difficult attending doctor.

"He is that bad," Everett said as if reading my own thoughts. "So for you to get stitch work is quite the compliment."

"I have to be honest, I was as surprised as anyone else when he stepped aside and invited me into his space. I thought it was a joke at first, or maybe a test of some kind, and worried a little that he'd reprimand me as soon as I moved over."

We left the stone path, our feet thumping on the wood planks of a pier that swayed slightly with our movement. "But you've got your own set of fans in the doctors." I said once we'd reached the end. Everett meant it when he said *short walk* because he sat down at the end and dangled his feet over the side. He patted the spot next to him until I moved to settle in.

"I do not have fans," he declared.

"Oh really? What about Dr. Niles, who never lets anyone answer questions except you because he insists he doesn't have time for wrong answers?"

"That's an intimidation tactic. He doesn't mean it."

Dr. Niles totally meant it, but I went on. "And what about Doctor Pearl, who has almost convinced me you should be sainted, knighted, and made administrator of the hospital."

He stiffened at Miss Pearl's name. "What has she said to you?" he asked carefully.

I bumped his shoulder with mine. "Nothing I don't already know about you. You really are a brilliant doctor. You're going to make the hospital of your choice very happy."

He held his breath and seemed to be waiting. When I didn't expound further, he asked, "Does she mention you when she's talking about me?" His voice cracked a little and he cleared his throat.

I stiffened as well. She talked plenty about me when talking about him, always making little observations on how I might feel for him. I laughed. "Well, if you count that she acts like she's some matchmaker working to make me fall in love with you, then yes. She mentions me a lot when talking about you." I laughed again, trying to make it seem like a joke.

He gave a thin smile but no laugh. My own laugh ended abruptly. We sat in the relative silence of the waves lapping gently into the bay.

Needing a quick change of subject, I asked, "Where are we exactly? The signs into the town of Camden were clear enough, but where is this?" I waved my hand over the water.

He leaned back on his elbows and said, "This is Penobscot Bay, home of the wealthy," he pointed to his neighbor's houses, "and the scrimped-and-saved-to-get-a-house-here." He pointed behind us to his own home. "But Grace likes it, and Dad likes what Grace likes, so this is where they live . . . all year long, even in the winter when it's wicked cold and miserable."

"What's your dad like?" I figured since Everett actually called his father *dad*, maybe there was a better relationship there.

"He's all right. Kind of a yes-man when it comes to my mom, but he's not too bad. He helped me with getting my bachelor's and didn't complain at all."

He didn't mention if anyone helped him with his medical schooling, and I decided not to ask. If his dad had helped him there, he likely would have mentioned it. We had a lot in common in that area. And even though our parents were polar opposites of each other, they were opposites in ways that affected Everett and me exactly the same.

We sat there in an easy companionship of the silent creak of the pier as the waves flowed around the bearing piles.

"I should let you get some sleep," Everett said after straightening and checking the time on his phone. "Riley has likely already shown up and is settled, which means we won't have to talk to her tonight. Tomorrow will be soon enough. And we'll both need sleep to handle her."

"Is Riley difficult?" I asked, thinking the daughter couldn't be more difficult than the mother.

"Riley is . . . interesting. Hazel is the only reason I care enough to keep any kind of contact with my family. You'll like Hazel. And since the weekend is to celebrate her, it shouldn't be too bad." He stood and held out his hand to help me up. I took it and squeezed his fingers a little. I don't know what I meant by the action, and I don't know how he took it, but he squeezed mine back and then released my hand.

He's got a girlfriend, I thought. *But he's here with me, not her.* That thought should have inspired some guilt, but it didn't, which *did* inspire guilt, but not nearly enough. I remembered back in the beginning when Everett held my hand after I got reamed by the dean at Boston University, how he hadn't let go and how that human connection had felt like it saved me somehow, that it tethered me to possibilities and hope.

I looked down at my hands, wishing he'd held on this time. But I was here. I had the weekend with him. I had his friendship and his respect as a peer. That would be enough.

Wouldn't it?

Chapter Fourteen

"Heels?" Grace eyed my footwear as if I'd entered their family kitchen where breakfast was being served in shoes covered in dog droppings.

"Tell me she isn't!" This came from a woman I assumed to be Riley—someone who hadn't even been properly introduced to me and yet who still felt okay about criticizing my shoes. Her eyes dropped to my feet. Everyone's eyes dropped to my feet—even my own. "And *scarlet*?"

"It's the very symbol of female bondage." Grace took a sip of her coffee with a shake of her head.

Where was Everett during this shark feeding frenzy? "Really?" I asked. "Because I always thought that female bondage was what happened any time a woman chose to do something because of how other people judged her rather than how she judged herself. And since I *like* heels and absolutely adore these shoes, it would seem more like my free will and choice rather than bondage, don't you think?"

And that was the beginning of breakfast.

They couldn't possibly have expected that I would somehow shrivel under their scrutiny. My grams always taught me to stand tall in my own shoes, to value my own opinion of self-identity, and not to cave to others. If standing taller in my own shoes could be literal as well as metaphorical, then all the better. When Grace and Riley realized they couldn't ruffle me, the subject was effectively dropped.

Everett's family was vegetarian and made a big pretentious show of being such, as if somehow I would be impressed or alarmed. I wasn't quite sure which reaction they wanted more from me.

Riley spread butter liberally over her toast. "We believe in eating pure in this household, so you won't find any bacon or eggs on our table for breakfast. I'm sorry if that disappoints you, but we're all vegetarians here." Riley said all of this as if she meant it to be an apology. But the words felt more like food supremacy than anything. Everett entered the kitchen just as she finished her little speech.

He opened his mouth, likely to tell her to lay off or whatever, but I cut in. "Since my mom's vegan, this vegetarian fare looks pretty amazing. You have a much greater variety here than I ever get at home. I mean, really, you actually have cheese, milk, and honey on the table. You even have butter."

Riley eyed me from under her blunt cut brown bangs, her eyes narrowed in a way that made her seem irritated with me for reasons I couldn't understand. She went on the attack first. Did she think I couldn't handle it? She'd inherited her mother's ice blue eyes and could give someone hypothermia from those eyes just as well as her mother. How nice to have a family super power.

Everett's warm hazel eyes came from his father. He didn't seem like an unpleasant person, but it was hard to tell since he hardly spoke during the meal.

Everett hustled me out to his car as soon as he could and apologized when we were shut up inside.

"Are they always like that?"

"Usually worse," he confessed. "They think picking on my houseguests is great sport, especially if those girls exhibit any traditionally feminine characteristics. I stopped bringing girls home a long time ago. I'm sure they went after you because of your shoes, which look very nice, by the way"

"Thank you." I looked at my feet and smiled at my heels. They really were fabulous. "Do you ever defend yourself, demand that they act like humans?" I asked after he'd turned onto the road.

"I was about to, but you handled yourself so well back there that I figured I'd just let you take care of yourself. Bravo, by the way. You shut them down fairly quickly. I've never seen anyone do that before."

Leaving the terrible-breakfast for the new social-good store felt a little pretentious—even if it had sprung up from his favorite sister's imagination. I'd felt more than surly toward the idea of a sibling who did social good when there was clearly so much familial good that needed to be done. If Hazel was anything like Riley, I was in for a messy day.

"Everett, I mean this is the nicest way possible. I would never let Riley defend me in a court of law."

He laughed and didn't stop laughing for several moments.

"I'm actually a little terrified to meet your other sister."

He flashed me a grin, one that said he understood exactly. But he said, "I already told you she was better than the rest of them."

"Yes, well, the others didn't exactly set the bar high, did they?"

Everett laughed some more. I joined in. The morning had been interesting. If I'd known something as innocent as footwear would cause such a stir, I might have done something really daring and worn my skirt with the laces that looked like a corset. We arrived at his sister's store, a place with balloons, food, and music from a local radio station. Hundreds of people crowded the parking lot.

And in all those people, Everett's other sister spotted us.

"Everett!" Hazel Covington appeared genuinely happy to see her brother. She was the first person aside from myself to show any enthusiasm toward him at all. His father had acted preoccupied, Riley had scoffed at him as if he was a bit of sun-worn plastic bag clinging to a barbed wire fence, and his mother had been indifferent to him—almost as if he hadn't sat at the breakfast table between her husband and me.

After the morning that felt more Twilight Zone than Brady Bunch, the moment Hazel said Everett's name with interest, I determined to like her and be her best friend. The little time spent with the rest of his family made me keenly protective of Everett. I wanted to drop-kick all his relations to the curb. His mom, I wanted to drop-kick twice, just out of principle.

But Hazel wasn't like the others.

She hugged her brother when she saw him, cooed over how fabulous he was to make such a long drive just for her, and then swept me up in the momentum of her greeting and hugged me too.

"He's told me all about you," she whispered in my ear. "You must be some kind of amazing, because he's never talked about any girl before."

For a moment, the comment made me anxious.

Did she think I was Liz—the girl he was really dating? What would she say when she found out Everett brought a stand-

121

in girlfriend? Would she be embarrassed for me? I felt a little embarrassed for myself.

"I think you might have mistaken me for someone else," I countered quietly, not trying to draw attention to the issue for anyone else.

Hazel laughed. "You *are* the doctor, aren't you? Everett's never mentioned anyone else, and I doubt he'd bring anyone else into the poorly done reality show that is our family."

I started at this news. I *was* the doctor. Not Liz. Liz was . . . I didn't even know what Liz was, but the only thing she did at the hospital was wait around for Everett and irritate me with her sweet smile and nice greetings.

"I'm Andra." I spoke with caution, just in case.

"Right," Hazel confirmed. "Andrea without the E."

I broke into a grin that could not be helped. Everett had made it abundantly clear that he didn't really like his family all that much—with the exception of Hazel. Mentioning me to the only sister he actually liked meant something important. He even told her the nickname he had for me.

The nickname thing was another point of interest. The Covington family did not use nicknames, but Everett had begun our relationship with a nickname. Maybe that was something he craved . . . a casual situation where things like nicknames and squabbling over who got the last donut in the box were normal instead of strange.

"Congratulations on your store," I said, finally feeling like coming all the way to Maine was a good idea. If I got nothing more out of this weekend than the knowledge that the only girl Everett ever spoke about was me, well then, mission accomplished.

"Thanks!" Hazel gushed. "In this day and age, to be able to open a brick and mortar store and have any hope at success is kind of rare. But this is my second store, and I can't tell you how excited I am!"

She had every reason to be excited. Her company, Second Childhood, made a comfort toy for a child in a third world country for every toy sold to a regular consumer in the first world countries.

Not only did the child in the third world country get a toy, but they also received a little picture book to begin an education.

The picture books varied depending on the target age of the toy, but all of them included health information on topics such as washing hands and brushing teeth in such an off-the-cuff way, the reader was not likely to know they were being instructed. Shoppers were welcome to buy the books in the store and they were also welcome to simply donate monetarily to the cause. Hazel boasted that every actual penny donated went straight to the source and not to pay any fat and lazy CEO.

Her store was charming, the kind any kid or kid-at-heart could get lost in. Even better, the prices were extremely reasonable, especially considering that when you bought something for your own kid, you were getting an identical item for a kid on the other side of the world. How did she keep such a business model afloat?

The name of her business, Second Childhood was genius since every purchase bought a "childhood experience" for two kids, not just one.

The press snapped pictures so often that I felt half-blinded by all the flashbulbs, even with the diffuser boxes on top of their cameras. I abandoned the crowd and tucked myself into a little nook with six child-sized chairs surrounding a child-sized table. I sat at the table with its fancy little porcelain tea set already arranged and smiled at the loveliness of it all.

"Two sugars, please." Everett smiled down at me and then sat.

"I don't remember sending you an invitation to my tea party," I said.

"That's because you only invited the stuffed shirts." He pointed to a large stuffed bear occupying the seat in between ours.

"Isn't that the point of a tea party? To invite people you don't really like so you can impress people who don't really matter?"

Everett grinned knowingly. "Your childhood really was as lame as mine."

I sighed and pretended to pour from the delicate tea pot. "Actually, when I was a very little girl, my mother was a big fan of tea sets. Before I had decided to enter the *masculine* world of surgery, we got along pretty well. She would sit with me and have tea parties using my tea set with real tea and real sugar and real cream." I made a soft tsking noise. "I really liked those moments back when we got along. I miss it."

"That sounds idyllic," Everett said and pretended to use the tongs to get us both sugars from the sugar dish. "I wish I had memories like that of my mom. It would make dealing with her a little easier."

"I don't know if it makes it easier or harder. Things like this remind me of all the ways I failed her in not being the shopping debutante daughter she really wanted. I always wonder if I could have been both the doctor and the debutante if she hadn't been so insistent that I chose only one." I poured me imaginary cream, but he put his hand out to stop me from pouring any in his cup.

"I don't take cream in my tea," he said quite formally.

I nodded and set the creamer jar down.

We picked up our respective saucers in one hand and removed the tiny cups from the saucers with our other. We even had our pinkies extended, as might have been considered proper.

"Well," Everett said. "Here's to your masculine profession."

We clinked our tiny cups together just in time for a flashbulb to go off and blind both of us. We blinked and scowled into the now spotty nook.

"Great picture. Thanks guys," the photographer said. "You can't stage them to look that natural."

He wandered off to presumably blind some other hapless victim.

Everett smiled at me. At least, I think he did. It was hard to tell through my spotted vision. "Why is being a doctor considered a masculine profession?" he asked.

For a moment I thought he was picking up the conversation his mother had tried starting both last night and at the breakfast table, but then he said, "Whenever I think of the word masculine, I always think of hairy chested, body builders. Most doctors—even the male ones, are usually quite thin and non-hairy . . ."

I laughed and could only drink my pretend tea and agree with him.

There were interviews by the media, punch and cookies—the real kind like you would give small children since it was a bookstore where actual children were wandering the store and choosing items their parents would hopefully buy for them.

The parents seemed willing to buy and happy to be there spending not only money, but also time, with their children. Whatever Hazel had done to spark interest in her company, she'd done it right. The whole affair was quite festive, and it made for a nice break in my study-work routine. According to the media, the patrons, and Hazel, the grand opening had been a smashing success and also created a lot of buzz for the online arm of the company, which celebrated its own spike in sales due to the attention.

The Covington family held a celebratory dinner party at their house on their back patio under a ceiling of twinkle lights with the ocean providing a steady soundtrack.

It would have been completely amazing if it had only been Everett, Hazel, and me. Sadly, the others had been invited as well. The three make-up free women faced each other around the dinner table as if gearing up for a death match of wits.

I sort of hoped that my burgundy lip gloss excluded me from the death match.

Riley seemed generally unhappy that her sister had experienced a great day and drew first blood.

"All you're doing with these stores," she said to Hazel as she plucked a roll from the serving dish, "is contributing to the world-wide landfill."

The statement made my jaw go slack, and I wondered if I should have brought an emergency doctor bag so I could tend the wounds they clearly meant to inflict on one another. But no one else seemed to notice the snark in the words, and Hazel didn't seem to mind at all. "That's not true. Most of our toys are considered to be of heirloom quality and heirloom desirability, which means they will be well-loved during their time with the original child, and then preserved and passed down to future generations."

"Who determines heirloom quality?" Riley asked. "And could someone pass the unsalted butter please?" She waved toward my end of the table where a pat of butter lay on a plate.

I hesitated a moment, unsure if the butter by me was the unsalted version she requested but when she waved again and rolled her eyes at me, I figured I didn't care which it was so long as it got her to turn her attention elsewhere.

Hazel smirked at her sister. "My research and development team make that determination. And since they're the best in the business, and I pay them a lot of money to stay smart, I'm inclined to trust them. And Dad, the asparagus is perfect, not too limp, not too crisp either. Just perfect."

"Thanks, Hazel," their father said. The normal word count in any sentence uttered by Gordon Covington was two. A long sentence consisted of three words.

But he smiled at his wife a lot, so I didn't think he was unhappy. His complacency served as his downfall in many ways. It kept him from being the kind of father who didn't allow his wife to henpeck her children and who didn't allow his children to henpeck each other.

Everett's parents had a complete reversal of roles in comparison to my parents. My mother was the quiet one smiling at her spouse. My father was the loud and demanding one who asked questions that had answers which could never satisfy him.

It was fascinating to watch from my point of view.

Fascinating and irritating.

Hazel had experienced a wonderful day. Why would her parents allow Riley to scorn the whole affair as if Hazel had done something socially criminal instead of socially good? Why would Grace continually make quips regarding Everett not being quite good enough?

A rush of relief flooded me when Riley excused herself from the table to use answer a phone call from a "very crucial client" and swept away with the grace of the dancer her mother likely scolded her to never become.

If heels were on the Covington documented banned list, surely ballet slippers would have been as well. I wondered what Grace would do if I showed up at breakfast in the morning with a tiara. I actually felt a bit of disappointed that I hadn't packed one. Oh well. Maybe next time.

At least "next time" if they ever invited me back and if I ever decided I wanted to partake in this live horror movie again.

As I sat, musing these thoughts and bouncing my one red-heeled foot, Grace settled her gaze on me. My bouncing foot halted and slowly lowered back down as I waited to see what she meant by scrutinizing me with such intensity.

"What kind of doctor are you studying to be?" she asked after a moment.

"A pediatric heart surgeon," I replied. "Like my father and my grandfather. It feels sort of like a family tradition, so it's a good thing I really enjoy internal medicine and children, both." I tried at a smile. So far, the conversation had gone well. Nothing dramatic or unfriendly.

"And your mother? Is she in the medical field as well?"

"No." I didn't elaborate since the chances of Grace approving of my mom's socialite behavior remained as thin as Grace's naked lips when she pressed them together at the onset of any displeasure. It wasn't that I cared if Grace approved, but more that I cared if the table of people continued biting at each other. People who invited contention to a conversation were people not worth knowing.

"Where do you hope to do your residency?" she asked.

"I'd like to stay in Massachusetts. I've grown used to it, I guess."

She fingered the napkin she'd placed next to her plate. "How are your grades?"

Hazel cut in and said, "If they aren't perfect, don't answer that. Nothing bugs Grace more than a woman who doesn't take her studies seriously. She grounded me once for a whole month over a C."

"I've got nothing to hide," I told Hazel. "They're not perfect, but I'm near the top of my class. So there's nothing to feel ashamed of."

"You hear that, Everett? The woman is the top of her class. It's not enough to bring a smart woman home, you should try to emulate her example."

Everett actually smirked at her comment. Smirked! As if his

mother hadn't basically called him stupid in front of the woman he'd brought home to meet the family.

"Actually," I cut in before Grace could lecture her son any further. "Actually, I'm only *near* the top of my class because Everett *is* the top of the class, and his grades and work ethic are insurmountable."

Everett stopped grinding pepper over his salad long enough to look startled at my comment. "That's not entirely true. My grades might be better, but Andra's work ethic is a thing of art." He winked and put the pepper grinder down.

How could he wink when the entire conversation made me feel so angry for him?

"Either way," Grace waved her hand through the air as if dismissing an unruly servant. "I'm glad you know what you're doing and where you want to be going, Andra. None of Everett's wild switching of schools in the middle and all that. He'll be lucky to get a residency at all with that kind of track record."

I tensed all my muscles to restrain myself from leaping up and screaming at the whole lot of them. "He's far more likely to get whatever residency he puts in for," I said, my voice surprisingly calm—even to me. "Everett is a commodity in the medical community." I'd intended on saying more, but Riley returned, and I fell silent instead. Everett wasn't bothered with their behavior. Why was I?

Riley continued her crusade to find fault with everything about the day and Hazel's success. Hazel laughed at half the things her sister said. Everett continued to smirk.

I kept quiet, letting them have their quarrels even while not understanding how the sibling group hadn't banded together the way Nathan and I had as children.

At least I kept quiet until Riley decided she'd had enough of picking on Hazel and turned her attentions to Everett.

"Done with nursing school yet?" she asked him.

I bristled at the comment—not because there was anything wrong with nurses or the nursing program, but because she meant the words to bite. My dad often suggested I study to be a nurse instead of a doctor since the lines between them blurred so much anyway, anymore.

"Almost," was the only reply Everett bothered to offer. I couldn't help the instinctive need to defend my position and to defend Everett's honor. But Everett must not have felt such a need. He didn't suck in a great breath of air like I had so that he could argue louder and longer than his sister. He didn't straighten as though someone had knifed him in the back.

He said one word.

Almost.

Why did it grate on me?

I should have stayed quiet. And I might have if Riley hadn't already worn me down by clipping snippets of Hazel's great day away and if Grace hadn't belittled her son just moments before and if the two of them hadn't messed with my heels this morning. But I *had* straightened and *had* sucked in the air, and there was nothing to be done for it except let it all out. "Why would you say that?" I asked.

The business of people eating meals at the table stopped and all eyes went to me.

"Say what?" Riley asked.

"Calling his education *nursing school* when you have to know he's in medical school to be a surgeon."

"Well, it's not like that's a bad thing, is it? Is there something wrong with being a nurse?" Riley petitioned the table.

Her mother shook her head, wide-eyed as if baffled by my impertinence.

I narrowed my eyes at her and set my utensils down. "Of course there's nothing wrong with being a nurse if that's what he was actually working toward. Just like there's nothing wrong with being a paralegal, but I'm willing to bet you'd get miffed if someone called you a paralegal because it downgrades the higher achievement, the longer stretch, as you well know, or you wouldn't have said it."

Hazel busted up laughing. "Go Everett! You've snagged yourself a girl who can hold her own at our family dinner table!"

I flushed deep and hot and remembered myself. I wasn't at

my house with my parents on one side of the dinner table and Nathan and me on the other side. This was Everett's family and I was a guest. "I'm sorry. This is your celebration dinner, and I'm probably out of line. I'm sorry," I said again. I wanted to get up and go to my room, but knew that would make me look like a coward to people who clearly despised weakness. And in reality, I wasn't sorry at all.

I stayed, and actually felt relief when Riley declared that she would never have a reason to support her sister's store because she never intended on having any children. It was hard not to feel relief. Maybe there was something to Grace's first declaration that some women weren't meant to be pigeonholed into the role of motherhood. Grace made a joke about kids not being so bad and actually urged Riley to reconsider as long as she only had one or two.

"Of course," Grace said with a laugh, "I'd only wanted two children, but a little too much wine and a little too few birth control pills contributed to me having to raise a boy, of all things." She stopped then and for the first time since meeting her, the woman actually managed to look a little embarrassed by what she'd said. Her mortification with herself made her a much more careful, somber human and dinner conversation turned into something almost friendly after that.

Everett took me on our short walk down the pier after dinner was put away and cleaned up. "Makes your family look normal, doesn't it?" he said as his feet slowly thumped against the planks.

"Is it always like that?"

"Naw." He laughed. "Sometimes it's worse." He took my hand when he realized I'd stopped to gape at him. "I'm just kidding. Sort of."

"How do you handle that?" I asked, still baffled. His family really did make mine look like a lakeside picnic. Whatever they were, I didn't mind that he had my hand in his, that he didn't let go.

"My mom had to get married—shotgun wedding situation. She resented a lot of things but most of all, she resented not becoming whoever it was that she wanted to be. Not that she couldn't have done whatever she wanted in life—even with children. But that she's afraid . . . really afraid, and she hides behind us and all the energy it took to raise us. We're kind of her convenient excuse to never try hard things. She took it out worst of all with Riley. She pushed Riley hard." We made it to the end of the pier and sat down; his hand dropped mine in the process of sitting, and he didn't take it again.

His mother would have scoffed my lack of feminism for not having the courage to take that initiative of hand-holding on my own, but knowing about her fears and insecurities made mine easier to feel okay with.

Everett continued, "I remember lots of nights lying in my bed, listening to Riley cry because she was so tired while my mom drilled her to *help* her get ready for a debate in school or when she made her give a talk over and over again to *help* prep her for the speech she needed to have memorized when she was running for student council. Things like that. I go easy on them because neither of them have been easy on themselves or on each other. It's all good."

I stared at him, the pale moonlight reflected in his face. "No. *You're* all good. The rest of us are kind of crap. I'm sorry I got involved. It wasn't my place."

Everett laughed. "Andrea without an E . . . that was the best dinner I've had with my family. It's nice to know you can hold your own with them. Like Hazel said, not many people can. You were brilliant."

"Does it bother you when they bite at you like that?"

He shrugged. "Probably. It's the way the family communicates and it's been going on for so long, I don't know anything else. My mom sometimes used to say that we may not like what she was telling us, but we always knew she was telling us the truth. She called them *kind truths*, which she insists are better than the apathetic lie."

I lay flat on my back on the pier and stared at the stars, which were few under the light from the full moon. "I've heard you say that before, but still don't get it."

He lay down next to me. "It means she loves us enough to be

kind and tell us the truth. If she was apathetic toward us, she would have told us a lie."

I turned to face him, propping my head up on my arm. "Sorry, I'm not buying it. Most of the things she says about you are absolutely not true, so it feels more like the apathetic lie."

He turned to me, mimicking my elbow prop. "Truth is perspective."

"Philosophy from a student of science. The scandal."

"The two are a genuine complement to each other. Yin and yang and all that."

I shook my head and laughed. "You are too good. Kind of disgustingly perfect. Have you ever done anything you shouldn't have?"

His face went from amused to intensely serious. "I invited you here this weekend."

I did not see that answer coming. "And that's bad because . . ."

"Because I sort of told a lie."

I wanted to make a joke, to tease him about telling a lie, to maybe ask him if it was an apathetic one or not, but the way the air emulsified with my every breath made such brevity impossible.

His confession came out in a tsunami of words. "I never invited Liz to come with me this weekend. She knew my sister had a store launch coming at some point and would have come if I had given her a specific time and date, but I didn't invite her because they would have eaten her alive." He jerked his head toward the lights flooding over the stone patio from the back windows of his childhood home.

"So you didn't invite her to protect her?"

He didn't answer right away, and I didn't know what else to do but wait, so I waited.

"Sort of," he said. "At first. But then as the time came closer, I knew I didn't want to come alone, and I was about to call her when you showed up, and then I knew I didn't want to come with anyone else . . . but you."

We stared at each other for an undetermined amount of heart beats. He didn't want to come with anyone else. He didn't want to come with anyone else. He wanted me to be with him.

His words were magnetized, pulling me in to him until I felt his breath on my face. "You didn't have to lie," I whispered. "I would've come either way."

A puff of breath passed over his lips, almost a gasp. Almost a sob. "You have no idea how long I've waited to hear you say that. How long I've waited for you to . . ."

I closed my eyes and leaned in to close the distance, to stop him from talking and to lose myself in the kisses that had become my fondest memory, but it seemed no matter how far I leaned, our lips never made contact.

I opened my eyes.

Everett had pulled away and sucked in air hard. "But Liz doesn't deserve this," he said.

I pulled back, too, snapped into reality with a truth that had to include a perspective beyond our own. "Right. Liz. Doesn't. I'm sorry." I started to get up, but his hand on my hand stopped me.

"Don't go. Not like this. Let me explain."

I felt insanely stupid and wanted to do the running I was used to doing when dealing with Everett. "Everett. There's nothing to explain. You have a girlfriend, and she's really nice. The last thing I want is to make some sort of Greg out of you so that Liz has an excuse to scrawl the word *TOOL* on your truck door. I just lost my head for a minute and you apparently lost yours too, but now we're both in the right frame of mind, so we can forget this . . ." I tried to wave my arms and perhaps shake his hand off mine, but he held firm. He remembered well enough all the times I'd bolted and wasn't about to give me that chance again now.

"Andra, I love you."

I stopped trying to stand and stared at him.

Why now? Why tell me that now after he'd refused a kiss and told me his girlfriend didn't deserve to be cheated on?

He continued once he realized I'd become a statue at the end of the pier. I couldn't even turn away from him and look out to the ocean where wild waves offered more stability than the hard wood planks beneath me. A breeze kicked in over the water's surface and a frothy chill over me.

"I'll break things off with Liz as soon as we get back."

Wait. What?

"You're . . . say that again?"

"I mean it, Andra. Being with the *wrong* person is just wrong. It's always been you. But I kinda gave up hope on you ever deciding on me again."

My head felt fogged over with too much. Just. Too. Much. "You can't do that to her. She'd be devastated."

"No, what I can't do is live a lie with her. She doesn't deserve to be cheated on, which is the only thing keeping me from you. But she doesn't deserve to be lied to, either. I'll come clean, and then you and I—"

"Can figure stuff out." I finished his sentence for him.

We were both on our knees smiling at each other over this new deal we'd just created.

"Yeah," he said. "We'll figure this stuff out."

In one swift motion, I leaned in and kissed his cheek. "That's a totally lame confession of wrong-doing. Next time, I expect to hear about you stealing a sticker from a kid you gave a shot to."

"I'll tell you about the time when I gave a shot to a kid who kicked me and I kicked him back." He helped me to my feet.

We walked to the house not touching each other, but warm with the potential of nothing barring our way in the future. How so much emotion could exist after so much back and forth staggered me. But it did. Maybe it was true when people said the third time's the charm.

Everett dropped me off at my door just down the hall from his. Our eyes were riveted to each other and I knew that Liz or no Liz, he had to go or I would end up kissing him. I gave him a little shove. "Goodnight, Everest without an S."

"Goodnight, Andrea without an E."

I finally felt like I could breathe once he'd moved down the hall. "Everett?" I whispered loud enough for him to hear, but hopefully not loud enough for anyone else."

"Yeah?"

"You didn't really kick a kid back, did you?"

He laughed. "I'll see you in the morning, Andra."

"Yes, you will." I whispered as I clicked my door shut behind me.

Chapter Fifteen

I awoke to the sound of a doorbell. My brain still fogged with dreams that had to have been pretty good, because I sighed a satisfied sort of sigh and smiled to myself while checking the time on my phone.

Just after ten.

How had I slept so late?

But I didn't mind so much. The sleeping-in luxury seldom showed itself to me. I was not one to look a gift horse in the mouth. With school almost over, a little relaxing made sense. But hanging out in my room when it seemed a whole life waited for me outside my door proved impossible. I dressed quickly and stuffed my belongings into my overnight bag in case Everett wanted to hit the road early to give us the day to spend time together, to talk and begin the figuring-out-of-stuff we'd talked about the night before.

Then I thumped down the stairs, feeling content and incapable of keeping another satisfied sigh from escaping me.

The sigh turned into a gasp when I hit the bottom stair. "Liz?"

I blinked, but she wasn't some figment of my imagination. She stood in the entryway.

She smiled at me, but her lip quivered, and her smile felt like daggers of shame to my heart. "Hello," she said. "Andra, isn't it? Andrea without an E?" Her eyes closed briefly a moment as if she could find some sort of inner strength inside her eyelids.

"Are you okay?" I shouldn't have asked. Alarm bells and the muffling sound in my ears meant adrenaline flooded my body, that same adrenaline that demands flight or fight.

I did neither.

Hardly anyone ever mentions the third option of adrenaline— the kind that actually affects most people and animals. It is not flight. It is not fight. It is fright. That fright that makes a deer stand in the way when headlights from a truck hurtle toward it. That fright held me to the spot on the bottom stair as Everett's girlfriend's lip quivered with a sadness that broke my heart.

Nothing happened, I could have said. But it would have been the kind lie. No, Everett hadn't let me kiss him—not on the lips anyway, but something had happened. He *had* confessed his love to me, and I had accepted that love.

Even my frosty, closed-off heart could not call such a confession and acceptance *nothing*.

Everett came down the stairs, led by Hazel, the two of them hissing rapid whispers at each other until they came into full view of the two women in Everett's life.

The whispers cut off as if sliced through with a blade.

"Liz . . ." he said.

Apparently that's all we had to say for ourselves. Her name. How eloquent.

Liz's gaze slid from me, to him, to Hazel. She tried at the smile again. "Congratulations on your new store, Hazel. I've heard all about it. I would've been there, but . . ." Her gaze slid back to Everett. "Well, I did get to see pictures of the launch on Facebook. A really great picture of Everett trying out a tea set."

Was I even breathing? Were any of us breathing? I could see everything from her point of view. I knew the moment of the tea set for what it was—another beginning of emotional floods. No one who witnessed that moment could have doubted how Everett and I felt about each other. And with the help of a photographer, there had been too many witnesses.

"Liz, I . . ." His voice from behind sounded like static in the muffled roaring of blood in my ears.

"Can we talk?" Liz asked, interrupting whatever Everett might have been trying to say.

"Sure. Sure. Let's . . ." He finished descending the stairs, next to me, then passing me entirely. "Sure," he said again. "How about outside. Let's go to the patio."

He moved to touch her back to help guide her to where the French doors led to the stone patio, but his hand hovered, never quite making the connection.

The door closed behind them.

Hazel descended the stairs as well and looked at me. "She said she's his girlfriend?"

I swallowed, not knowing what words to say. I nodded.

Hazel grunted and gave me a hug. "Don't think this is how I am. I hardly ever hug anyone, but I'm working on being more open to people's energy. Your energy is screaming for reassurance right now, so let me give it to you. Everett has never mentioned this girl. Not once. And honestly, the way she stood on the porch like a frightened mouse means my mother will act like a hawk in search of a meal if she ever meets her. You're okay. Girlfriend title or not, only one girl here has his heart. I would stay and give life advice all day, but I have to go to the store. You okay? You got it?"

I nodded some more.

But I didn't have *it*, whatever it was. Was I a bad person? Nothing happened. Everything happened. Were we wrong? I didn't know and hated not knowing. I finally forced myself down from that bottom step. I rounded the banister railing and came in full view of the couple outside through the windows.

In an odd detached kind of way, I watched, like watching a movie, or a play performed for me alone. Liz was a lovely crier. Nothing snotty or messy about it, just perfect round tears rolling down slightly flushed cheeks. Her wet lashes darkened with the tears, making her eyes seem brighter than before. A dull ache sucked my breath from me when his arms wrapped around her and her head went to his shoulder as he tried to comfort her. She held him hard, like she might never let go.

Nothing happened.

Everything happened.

It was time to leave.

I called a cab.

Cabs in Maine moved with a much higher respect for time than they did in Massachusetts because the yellow vehicle idled in front of the door almost before I'd returned from grabbing my already-packed bag from my room.

I looked back to the patio. Liz still held Everett. Everett still held Liz. I gripped the leather handles of my overnight bag and stepped onto the front porch.

Maybe we could sort it out later. Maybe he would tell her the truth, kind or apathetic, and she would have her disappointment and everything would be okay for us.

I transferred from the cab to the train station, where I boarded the Amtrak to Massachusetts. It was after the train released its brakes and rolled forward that a text came.

I expected to see Everett's name in the tiny screen, not my brother, Nathan's. The words all in caps fuzzed through my already clouded mind.

COME HOME NOW. IT'S GRAMS. SHE'S SICK.

The Fourth Chamber

Seven Years Later

The red string of fate may stretch or tangle, but it will never break.

—Chinese Legend

Chapter Sixteen

Grams suffered a heart attack. I arrived at the hospital barely in time to hold her hand, feel her soft fingers on my face, and whisper a sobbing goodbye as the red line on the monitor spiked lower and lower and lower and then not at all.

For all the knowledge of the heart we had in our family, we were helpless to keep hers from stopping.

I don't know what happened after that. Not really. I know I graduated medical school, my fingers reaching for the necklace that wasn't there. My heart reaching for the person who wasn't there.

The one thing I remember with any clarity was Miss Pearl. She had grieved with me in a way that no one else seemed to be capable. At graduation, she patted my cheek, much like my grams would have if she had been there to do so, and she said, "I must go and help others now. I can see you need time to marinate in your current situation before you're ready. But when you *are* ready, you can guarantee I will be there. I won't forget your heart, Andra Stone."

But what good were emotional hearts? I threw all my focus in the only kind of heart I knew how to save: the physical heart. And the loss of Grams proved I didn't even know how to save that one.

Humans have an innate sense of rhythm; from the very beat of our hearts, the lifetime companion of every man, woman, and child is a constant cadence keeping time of the seconds—even the ones missed while we're not looking.

My entire time in residency was spent not looking.

I did my residency at Massachusetts General. I don't know where Everett did his. I can't remember ever saying goodbye to him, or saying anything to him really. He never called or broached communication of any meaningful kind. The static fuzz in my ears that began with Liz at the bottom of the stairs never really went away.

I finished my residency, received my board certification in pediatrics, and went to complete my surgical residency at the Boston Children's hospital—the place I had wanted to work all along, the place Everett and I had discussed as our top pick all those years ago in study groups where I never saw him because I'd been looking in the wrong direction.

After surgical residency, I was hired on as a pediatrician specializing in cardiology. I hoped to be able to work my way up to surgeon.

I half-expected to see Everett the first day of work at Boston Children's. But he never turned up. With the extreme passage of time, he likely was married with a mortgage, a dog, and a child or two.

I dated.

I even liked some of them.

I even liked some of them a lot.

But when it came time to commit, I reached in to find my heart to give it away and found that it was simply missing.

So I'd become a frosty tyrant after all. But not too frosty. I bought toys for my favorite patients and for patients who weren't even mine but who I felt needed a pick-me-up.

Of course, I bought the toys from Hazel Covington's online store, Second Childhood, figuring the purchases to be a win-win since the toys I bought went to sweet children in need in my hospital and also paved the way for other toys to go to sweet children in need on the other side of the world. Boston Children's motto was *until every child is well*. I took it a step further and figured until they really were well, they were mine. I took care of them accordingly.

Shortly after I stopped one of the other physicians from giving painkillers to a young patient who'd suffered an aneurysm, a new position opened up at the hospital. The physician had been fired for the negligence that could have turned out very badly. His error came from the fact that he'd given in to the temptation of indulging in narcotic pain killers for himself. His addicted mind reasoned that pain killers were the answer to everything. But they were *not* the answer to a brain aneurysm. How would we gauge the teen's ability to think if her head had been glazed over with drugs known to cause hallucinations?

We were short-staffed with the firing of that physician, and a new-hire was sorely needed. I ached with the length of time the administration took to interview and search out a reasonable replacement that could be sufficiently vetted for the insurance companies and had all the appropriate background checks done. I ached because it seemed I never went home or got a break.

I ached even more when the replacement showed up.

Everett, like a poltergeist pulled from my past, stood in the hall of my hospital and stared at me as if he, too, saw a ghost.

Everest without an S.

He blinked at me until a voice from farther down the hall called out, "Doctor Covington, if you'll follow me."

He was gone again. My mouth hung open, caught somewhere between greeting him and stammering out some pathetic noise.

"What was that all about?" Becca asked. She eyed me and then eyed the two figures disappearing down the hall.

Becca had quickly become my favorite nurse. Her sassy attitude of flipping her curly blonde hair when doctors or patients gave her grief, and her uncrackable calm, even under the worst emergency situation, made her everyone's favorite, but she'd also become my best friend.

Becca was the girl I called when my brother made it onto The Food Network's show, Chopped. She watched it with me, threw popcorn at the screen when Nathan's rivals were back-biting monsters, and jumped up and down with me screaming when Nathan won. Becca went to concerts with me, even when they were classical music concerts, but more especially when they were her favorite band, Mystic Planets. Becca laughed at the fact that the hospital expected me to keep people alive even when I couldn't seem to manage to keep any of my houseplants alive. The fact that she had a not-so-secret crush on my brother meant that maybe I'd land the girl as a sister.

In spite of all that, Becca witnessing my first encounter with Everett made the entire thing worse and more confusing to me. When I didn't answer, she rounded the corner of the nurse's station, crossed her arms over her Winnie-the-Pooh scrubs and narrowed her eyes at me. "Maybe you didn't hear me ask, so I'll do it again since I'm accommodating like that. What was that all about?"

"I don't know."

"You don't know, or you don't want me to know?"

"Both. Neither. I don't know."

Her eyes suddenly went from narrowed slits to wide, mascara-framed moons. "Is that the guy?" She spun to look down the hall again, though Everett and Doctor Ferran were well beyond visual range. "Is it? THE guy? The one you take a second helping of ice cream over whenever we watch romantic comedies? Is he that guy?"

"No." I flustered. "I don't even know what you're talking about."

Her mouth fell open, and she started to bark out some kind of laugh. "It is! He is!" She whisper-yelled in the way only Becca could pull off. "That's second-helping-ice-cream guy!" She grabbed my arm and began to shake it as if she was a child trying to get her mother's attention. "I can't believe it! Here! In our hospital! This is the most exciting thing to happen, since . . . I don't even know. Nothing this exciting has ever happened."

I peeled her off my arm and scowled. "This is not exciting. This is a disaster. I'm over it. He's over it. There's no reason for anything to be brought up again now."

"Hm." She raised a brow at me, mocking me with the ability because I still couldn't do it and she looked crazy fabulous when she did it. "Sounds like denial. If you're both so over it, why would you think it'll come up?"

I hung my head in my hands and wondered if I was going to throw up. Or maybe pass out. Maybe both. "I don't know. That door closed a long time ago. I'm not prepared to deal with the reality of it, that's all."

She gave me her pity-sigh, the one that was long and sad, like a foghorn from a lighthouse. "Well, maybe this is a new opportunity. You know what they say: when one door closes, another one opens."

I moved my hands from my face to glower long and hard at my friend. "And you think that's supposed to make me feel better?

That somehow a bunch of doors opening and closing means I've got opportunities? Doors closing and opening isn't the sign of an opportunity, it's the sign of a haunted house! I am being haunted. Everett Covington is my own personal poltergeist." I growled and buried my face in my hands again.

"Maybe that's the answer." Becca tugged on a curly, blonde wisp that had strayed into her eyes and moving it back behind her ear.

I peeked between my fingers. "An exorcism?"

She groaned and pulled my hands from my face. "No. If you feel haunted by it, that means there's something still there, something you can't let go of. If you face this and either embrace it or get over it, then maybe you'll be a better date for those poor saps stupid enough to ask you out."

I stared at her a long moment. She smiled with the encouragement that could not have come from anyone else.

But I wasn't feeling encouraged. "You think I'm a bad date?" I asked.

"Sweetie, you know I love you, but you are thirty-five years old. You need a man before the hours of this place grays your head and wrinkles that cute face of yours so you look like a moldy apple someone left in the break room."

"I'm not thirty-five yet." I said.

Becca put her hand up to halt my protest on my tongue. "You're closer to thirty-five than you are to thirty-four."

I conceded the point by asking, "What do I do?"

She tilted her head to the side and gave me that look—the mischievous one that would have meant trouble if we were both younger and less responsible. "Is he cute?"

"How would I know?" I said too fast and with too much defense in my tone. "I only saw him for a second in the hall."

"Okay so not just cute, but hot." She knew me too well for our own good. "A hot new doctor who is likely to be the new meat around all the single ladies in this place means you had better stake a claim and stake it fast. Some of these women are desperate."

"Well, I'm not one of them, so I don't need to stake a claim." But my heart quickened at the mention of the other women in the hospital—pretty, intelligent, talented women. Would Everett date one of them? Would I have to watch him date someone else all over again?

Argh! And why did I care if he dated? We were over. The deed was done. That chance was gone when his arms went around Liz to offer her comfort and when there was no one to offer me comfort when Grams died. Done!

We were done.

And I'd made my peace with that, hadn't I?

"Dr. Stone?" Another nurse drew my attention from Becca and the puzzle of Everett.

"Yes, George?"

"The Baker girl is prepped and ready."

I checked my watch and nodded. "Right. I'll be right in. Thank you." I existed in this hospital to be a doctor, and Everett or no Everett . . . *that* was what I was going to do.

The decision would have been easier if Becca hadn't smirked and waggled her eyebrows at me.

I didn't see Everett again for the rest of the day, though I dreaded every moment for fear of what I would say to him when we came face to face again. What could we say? What if he wore a wedding ring? Worse, what if the woman he called Mrs. Covington was Liz? Liz would not like seeing me again. Not that I wanted to see her either.

The last time Liz and I made eye contact had been the single worst day of my entire life. Even thinking about that woman and that day filled me with so much sadness I wondered if I could drown in it. I went home that night and streamed movies from the internet and could not recall a single one of them.

I didn't see Everett the next day either. He hadn't been in the clinic seeing patients yet, though there was a general buzz of gossip and speculation about him among the staff. I heard him called handsome, intelligent, funny, charming, and arrogant—though that comment came from Rachel who didn't like doctors much, since, as a nurse practitioner, she felt she had as much experience as we did, and not nearly half the respect.

Where were they hiding him? It's not like our department was so huge that a new hire was impossible to introduce to the rest of the staff—at the very least to the other doctors.

The third day I turned a corner and there he was, right in my face, close enough to see the shift in his eyes as they went from brown to green to gold to brown again. He smiled at me, his eyes warm, his smile gentle. "Andrea without an E. I wondered where you'd been hiding."

"I haven't been hiding. I've been working." I didn't return the nickname greeting. It simply felt too intimate, too personal, too hard to push past my lips. He must have noted the omission because he raked his hair back with his fingers—that nervous habit I knew so well.

He used his left hand, and I should have been ashamed of myself for straining to really see those fingers as they glided back through his dark hair, but I couldn't help it. Sometimes, a girl just has to know.

His ring finger remained bare, and the tightening in my chest eased up much more than I cared to admit. The problem came when my mouth finally opened to speak and the only thing blurted out were the words, "So, you're not married?"

The mental face-palm was hard enough to give me phantom pain in my forehead.

His smile widened, just a fraction. "I'm not. Couple of almosts, but in the end, my heart wasn't really in it, so nothing worked out."

"I'm sorry," I said as the words *not sorry* did a dance in my gray matter.

"You?" He raised his brow with a look that made me worry he could see my *not sorry* dancing in my mind.

"Same. Couple close calls, no results. Becca jokes I'm married to my job, but when she does, Nathan jokes I'm really married to the idea of irritating our mother by denying her grandchildren. Since Nathan and Becca are likely to actually get together, my mom can get grandchildren through them, instead."

I was talking too much.

"How is Nathan? I saw him when he won Chopped. That was pretty amazing. And who's Becca?"

Everett had watched my brother on Chopped.

That he cared enough to stay connected through that small detail pinged my heart, forcing me to shake myself into reality and realize he'd asked me a question. "Becca? She's a nurse here. You'll come to love her when you get to know her. There isn't anyone more competent or trustworthy. Actually, the whole staff is pretty great."

He leaned his head to the side and outright grinned. "They say the same thing about you. And I hear, I owe you a debt of gratitude."

"Gratitude? For what?"

"Your quick thinking and interference with another doctor's exam of an aneurysm patient led the administration to realize that doctor had a problem. I only work here now because you helped them see that he shouldn't work here."

Which was all just a nice way of his saying I got that other doctor fired. "Doctor Wyatt's termination wasn't my doing. He got himself fired by writing himself out prescriptions for narcotics," I informed Everett so there was no question of how everything really happened.

"He got himself fired, yes. But you kept him from getting fired by actually causing harm to a patient."

"Oh . . . well, anyone would have been able to do the same thing. I just happened to be in the vicinity when they brought her in." We'd been standing a long time, doing nothing but talking, and we weren't even talking about anything that had to do with any of the important things I imagined we ought to be discussing. I stepped to the side to move past him and remove myself from the awkward situation. "Well, it's great to see you. I'd better get back to work. Gotta finish rounds and get back to the clinic for appointments."

"Right. Me too. Appointments."

We both flashed smiles, his looking as nervous and baffled as mine felt and we moved around each other.

Before I made it three steps away, he said, "Hey, Andra?"

I turned, but not enough to encourage a great deal more of that awkward conversation. "Hm?"

"How are you, I mean, it's been what? Six years? How are you, really?"

Six years. It had been six years.

"I'm fine. Good. Living the dream." I almost turned entirely away again, but hesitated before finally asking, "And you? How have you been?"

He appeared startled to have me ask the question. "Good, I guess. I . . ."

I had no manners, hadn't asked after his life, or asked about his family. With an inward sigh, I forced myself to face him directly again, to make myself have a civil conversation. We would see each other often, and beginning the relationship well would make it easier in the future. "Where did you do your residency?" I asked.

"Johns Hopkins."

We discussed residencies, and pros and cons between the two hospitals as well as the pros and cons of the hospital we stood in at that moment.

"I'm glad things have been good for you, Everett. You deserve good things."

He raked his fingers through his hair again. "You too. I've thought about you a lot over the years. I've missed you."

Not again. Not again. Sweet mercy, not again. I couldn't fall into the cyclone one more time. I also couldn't drag him into the cyclone. It wouldn't be fair to either one of us.

I turned my smile up to "bright" the way I did with worried parents when they brought their children in for testing. I was surprised how much of my job consisted of comforting worried parents. "Well, it looks like we're both good. Things worked out, and we're right where we belong."

"Exactly. Right where we belong. Standing in front of each other. Again."

That hadn't been what I meant. I meant we were right where we belonged separately, not together. But to refute him would mean saying words my mouth couldn't seem to form. Instead, I ducked my head and said, "Well, see you around then."

My feet didn't need encouragement. They fled the scene, dragging my traitorous heart along with them. Everett was back. How would I ever survive such a universal glitch in my life?

Getting back to the clinic felt like returning to a refuge. I collected my wits in my office and forced myself to focus. I had several patients who needed my time today to be about them, not about silly matters of ex boyfriends.

I laughed at that.

Yes. Ex boyfriends. The plural form totally counted with Everett. We'd gotten together three times and broken up just as often. Fate had a terrible sense of humor for throwing this guy in my path over and over again.

Finally feeling collected enough to be of use to my patients, I exited my office.

And ran right into Miss Pearl.

Chapter Seventeen

"Seriously?" I did not mean to say it out loud, but seriously?

How could this woman, of all the people on the planet, turn up outside my office just moments after I had the most awkward, uncomfortable conversation in my entire life. It wasn't bad enough that Everett showed up again with his *I miss you*'s and his smile that made my stomach flip whether I wanted it to or not, but his greatest administrative advocate had to show up as well?

"I'm also glad to see you, Doctor Stone," she declared. "I take it, you've adjusted well to life as a doctor?"

"Yes. Thank you." The question reminded me of how she had been there for me during the death of my grandmother. She wasn't just an advocate for Everett, she'd been an advocate for me, too. To think of her in any other way was unfair. "How have you been, Miss Pearl?"

"Quite busy. The heart business is a lot of work sometimes." She passed a hand over her eyes and looked tired in way I hadn't ever seen her appear before.

"Are you okay?"

She smiled. "I really am glad to see you, Andra."

And that did it. Her calling me by my first name instead of calling me Doctor Stone melted any resolve I had. I wrapped my arms around her and gave the woman a hug. "And I'm really glad to see you. Sorry for seeming startled at first, but I was . . . well . . ."

"Startled?" she asked.

I laughed and pulled away. "Yes. Exactly that. So what have you been up to? What brings you to Boston?"

She shrugged. "Same thing as usual. Broken hearts needing fixing."

She certainly had a way of putting things. I looked at her and realized that she hadn't aged at all. She seemed maybe fifty years old when we'd met the first time. That was six years ago. Not a single gray hair, not a single wrinkle at the corners of her eyes. I wanted to ask her what skin care system she used because clearly, it worked miracles.

"Where are you off to, Miss Andra?" she asked.

I checked my watch. "Appointment. And I should really get to it. Daniel's parents are likely to give the kid a donut if I keep him waiting too long because they're afraid he'll get bored."

"A donut doesn't sound too bad," Miss Pearl said.

"It is when you're dealing with childhood obesity and hypertension as a ten year old."

"Then I'll see you later," she offered, giving me a warm pat on the cheek before disappearing down the hall.

Yes, that was what Miss Pearl did best. The hospital Houdini.

I wondered throughout the day why she'd come to my clinic and hospital. Did someone else get fired? Or maybe someone was going to? Or, more likely, someone was about to retire and—

I halted in the hallway in front of the check-up room.

Maybe a surgeon was retiring?

Maybe a heart surgeon.

Half the surgeons were pretty old, of retirement age, where they would be turning their eyes to enjoying the fruits of their many years of labor in the hospital. And if one of them retired, then it meant a position would be opening up. Perhaps Miss Pearl arrived to choose a new surgeon.

I hoped as I'd never hoped before, even though it was just as likely I'd made the entire scenario up and no one planned to retire at all; and Miss Pearl was merely here to help with the hospital's scheduling or whatever.

Maybe I would get the chance to be a surgeon sooner than I'd hoped.

Maybe.

I went in to Daniel's appointment with a far better attitude than ever before and was able to coax his parents to commit to a diet plan that would help their son control his blood pressure and keep his ticker tocking longer and more effectively. They also grudgingly agreed that removing the TV from their son's bedroom might encourage him to leave his room every now and again, and perhaps go outside and get some exercise instead. This admission was a breakthrough of huge proportions, since his parents wanted me to fix the symptoms, not the problem.

They agreed that the hypertension their son experienced at so young an age gave legitimate cause to worry. The kid experienced problems that most people didn't suffer well into late adulthood. Daniel's pleasant demeanor and general sweetness would likely lead to friends if he could just get outside long enough to make them. Getting outside might get him into building a tree house, or playing a sport.

My next patient was Clarissa, one of the most beautiful children I'd ever laid eyes on. Her dark curls framed an oval face, blue eyes, and a ready grin, even with the fact that she suffered from a myxoma, a tumor in her heart. We discovered the tumor after her parents brought her in as a last effort to understand their daughter's chronic and debilitating fatigue. They'd been to doctor after doctor and none of them could ever figure out what made the little girl so exhausted all the time.

At the time they brought her to me, I listened to their story, read her charts and immediately set her up for the tests necessary to check on a blockage in her heart. They found it on the right side, and we referred her to Dr. Mendenhall for surgery.

I took care of her post op recovery and felt elation at the girl's energy levels.

That night, I didn't go home, but instead collected the packages that had arrived in my office and took them to visit the rooms of patients who were set up as residents of our hospital—those kids with terminal illnesses. A ballerina doll and a bear in a super hero cape had shown up, and I knew just who needed them.

The two children slept as I crept into their rooms and delivered their presents along with a note to them filled with positive messages.

Only after the presents were quietly delivered did I go home and think about Everett going home. Where did he live? He couldn't have had a girlfriend there waiting for him, or he wouldn't have told me he missed me.

Well . . . that might not be true either. He had told me all sorts of things when he was dating Liz. That thought helped put my mind back in order. I wasn't going there again. I would not tangle myself up in all things Everett.

I wouldn't.

I firmly made that decision when I found myself thinking about him while I stirred the pasta in the pot of boiling water.

I resolutely made the decision again while grating fresh parmesan over my plate and imagining him teasing me for insisting on fresh parmesan.

I definitely made the decision when getting ready for bed and thinking of how I felt the night we'd decided to work things out.

After all those decisions, I firmly, resolutely, definitely made the decision that I had no sense of actual resolve. I yanked down my bedspread and sheets, got into bed, and covered my head with a pillow so I could scream into it.

Weeks later, I found that my path crossed very seldom with Everett's. My path hardly crossed with Miss Pearl's, as well. So, despite all the change I'd imagined finding with the two people reentering my life, nothing had changed at all.

Not really.

But it felt like everything had changed. I dressed with a little more care in the morning in case Everett bumped into me in the halls or the cafeteria. I sought out opportunities to be where Miss Pearl might be so she could see how hard I worked and be impressed by my ethic. And I worked like a dog.

If a surgeon position came available, I wanted to be high on the list of candidates.

Because of the minimal interaction between Everett and me, the day he sidled up to me in the cafeteria and whispered, "Hey, Andrea without an E," my skin goose-pimpled and my face went to the temperature of the sun.

"Everett! What are you doing here?"

He grabbed a tray and put it down in front of him. "I came to eat lunch with my favorite doctor."

"You don't get out much if I'm your favorite," I said.

"I've spent the last seventeen years of my life with doctors. I think I get out plenty." He pulled a pudding off the shelf in the chilled glass display cases.

I made myself a salad from the salad bar, waiting for him to say something else, something that would explain his presence, the nearness of him, the sudden companionable attitude when it seemed he'd spent the month previous ignoring me.

When he didn't say anything more, I pointed at his tray and gave him my best lecture-look. "Is that really your lunch?"

Looking sheepish, Everett hurried and made himself a salad as well. At the last moment before it was our turn to pay in line, he also grabbed an apple crisp dessert.

We sat down together at a table and he still hadn't really said anything, so I began eating my salad. He watched me a moment, but I refused to be intimidated by Everett Covington. He invited himself to my lunch, he certainly had to expect that eating would be involved.

When my lunch tray neared total emptiness, he finally spoke up. "So Hazel is coming into town, and I was wondering if you were going to be available while she was here."

"Hazel's coming?" I blinked at Everett, uncertain why his sister's visit was a matter of concern to me.

"Yes. She caught whiff of a rumor that one the doctors at Boston Children's makes frequent purchases from her website."

Had my face felt warm before? Now it felt steamy enough to melt off and drip onto the floor. "Oh."

"Exactly. Oh, indeed." He nodded. "Turns out, lots of toys are delivered to this address. Naturally, Hazel is interested. She's coming with a donation to the hospital to thank that doctor personally."

We stared at each other a long minute over our lunch trays. "How did you know?"

"You're kidding, right? Hazel's my sister. On occasion, I spend time in her toy store while I'm waiting for her. That's a lot of browsing time when you're waiting on the owner to get out of an endless line of meetings. I think I know her product line better than she does. So when most of the rooms in this hospital have my sister's toys sitting their stuffed bottoms on patient's beds, I put two and two together and called Hazel to see if there was a way to track how many packages were delivered to the hospital over the last few months. When she saw how many, she realized she had an opportunity to do some local social good. Your credit card must be maxed out, Andra."

I bit my lip and tightened my hands on my mug of hot chocolate, letting the heat seep into my fingers. "I . . . uh, actually use the money from my inheritance. Grams was very generous to me. I carry no debt of any kind."

Everett's brow creased ever so slightly, and his jaw tightened with my confession over who *really* paid for the toys. "I'm sorry, Andra. I'm so sorry about your grams. I didn't know until the funeral was over and I didn't know what to say or how to make anything right or how to fix what was so incredibly broken. I am so sorry."

"It's water under the bridge, Everett. It's done, past, no longer an issue."

His hand flinched like he meant to grab my hand. Instinctively, my hand flinched as well, preparing to dodge any such attempt. The conversation stripped me to raw vulnerability and I wanted to be gone, away from Everett and his apologies that came years too late, and the aching emptiness that swallowed me every time I thought about my grandmother.

Everett did not grab my hand.

I did not flee.

"I won't ask you to forgive me, Andra. Not trying to contact you as soon as things settled with Liz was unforgivable, I know that. But I wanted you to know that I was sorry. So incredibly sorry."

Part of me wanted to ask how long exactly it took to settle things with Liz and wanted to ask why he hadn't contacted me; the other part of me wanted to rant mad-woman-style about the horror of going through Gram's death alone and how he could have been there for me if he'd wanted to.

The third part of me was the part that won.

I forced a smile to my face. "There's nothing to forgive. We had our own struggles to deal with back then. Everything worked out how it was supposed to, and we're both fine."

Not fine. Not exactly.

"You can be the better person and go easy on me if you want to, but I know what I did wrong and can feel guilty and sorry if I want to."

I raised my hand to indicate he could do as he wished and changed the conversation back to something that didn't splinter and fracture my heart like thin ice in a spring melt. "I don't think the hospital will be thrilled with a bunch of PR hoopla. Are you sure Hazel coming is such a great idea?"

"Who's Hazel?"

Everett and I both looked up to see the new visitor to our table. "Becca, hey . . . what are you doing?"

She sat down without waiting to be invited. "Eavesdropping like the good friend I am. Who's Hazel and why won't admin like her?"

"Becca," I said, "have you met Dr. Covington?"

She smiled wide for Everett. "I do work here, don't I?"

I laughed.

Everett did as well. "Becca has been unlucky enough to be forced into giving me frequent tours when I get turned around in this place."

Becca swept back her blonde curls and waved at both of us as if shooing away any side conversations she had no interest in. "So what hoopla? What Hazel? What admin?"

"Admin will be fine," Everett assured us both. "In fact, the whole thing was almost their idea. Miss Pearl said that with our excellent recovery rate in cardiology, this other exposure will bring nothing but good to the hospital for all the other departments as well. I made sure to clear it with anyone who might object before I greenlit the project."

Becca buttered her roll. "What project?"

"The Grandmother Foundation," I said at the same time Everett said, "The Heart Stone project."

We both flashed surprised glances at each other. "You made this a *project*?" I asked.

"Did you actually create a foundation?" he asked. Then we laughed together, and Becca smiled like she'd been let in on a secret no one else knew about.

"Yes," I said. "I created a foundation with my inheritance. I wanted to spread her love a little." My eyes blinked back the tears and the back of my throat burned and tightened. "It seemed like the right thing to do."

"It sounds pretty right to me," Everett agreed. "And to answer your question, yes, Hazel made this a project. Once I told her of Miss Pearl's idea of making it something bigger, something that we could invite other people to participate in, she grew the whole thing from one event to something that would be ongoing."

Becca smacked her hands on the table demanding our attention. "I'm still lost, people. It's kinda hard to butt in to a conversation if those conversing refuse to provide backstory. How about filling me in?"

Everett explained his sister, her business, and my quietly giving gifts to the children of the hospital."

"You really do that?" Becca asked.

"He makes me sound far more heroic than I really am," I insisted.

"And you never invited me to play? I would have helped." She looked actually sad that I hadn't ever included her.

"Well, you're invited now," Everett said. He turned back to me. "So are you on board?"

"I'm not really sure what this is," I confessed.

He shrugged. "It's a couple interviews, some video footage of you at work, and your approval of the media being shared."

"Of course I will if I'm really needed, but wouldn't it be better to have someone in admin take care of it? Someone like Miss Pearl? She has tons of personality and charisma and would be great in an interview."

Everett laughed. "Miss Pearl actually flat out refused to be a part of any interviews. She said if anyone puts a camera in her face, then she will put a slap on their face. She sounded sincere. I think we should believe her."

Becca nearly spit out her food as she laughed at the mental image of Miss Pearl slapping a cameraperson.

"So will you?" Everett asked me again.

I agreed, wondering what it was I was getting myself into.

Everett, apparently feeling like his work was done, dug into his dual desserts of apple crisp and pudding.

I stared at him until I had the feeling someone was staring at me. I turned to Becca. She smiled and slid her glance to him, then back to me. She mouthed the word *hot*. She even fanned herself, then jabbed a thumb at him, which made me scoot my chair back abruptly and grab hold of my tray. I did not want to be around for Everett to see her mentally setting us up together.

Everett stood as well. "You're leaving?" he asked.

I glanced at Becca, who rolled her eyes. "I've got an appointment." I wasn't even sure if the words were true or not, just sure that I didn't want my best friend flirting with my serial-ex-boyfriend on my behalf. "Go ahead and finish your lunch. I'll talk to you both later."

I hurried away before Becca could do or say anything that would make my ear-tips burn. She'd likely do and say plenty, but at least I didn't have to witness any of it.

I ran into Miss Pearl on my way to my office. She smiled wide at me and said, "We're done marinating, aren't we? It's definitely time, Andra. I can see it in your eyes."

"Time for what?" I asked.

"I told you I'd come back when you were ready. And I think you're finally there."

"Finally there?" My heart rate quickened. "Are we talking about a job?" Maybe the position for surgeon was already open. Would they have opened it without any of us knowing?

She started walking toward my office; I followed along since I was going that direction anyway. She pressed her lips together before opening them again to reply, "For *my* job, yes. I need you to spend some time with Dr. Covington, to help him feel welcome here at the hospital."

"He's been here a month. If he doesn't feel welcome by now . . ."

"I want him to feel like we're taking a personal interest in him, to make sure he belongs and that he's planning on staying with this new situation for the long duration."

The long duration?

Did she mean for Everett to take the new surgeon position?"

"I also want to make sure his sister has everything she needs while she's visiting. You will be very important in bringing some wonderful media attention to this hospital and to the cause of children's needs everywhere."

"About that . . ."

"I know," she interrupted before I could form the words. "You wanted those gifts to be something done privately, but I believe you have a cause here bigger than you can imagine. You and Dr.

Covington will be quite a team, quite a force for good in a world of exhaustion."

We were at my office.

She patted my arm. "I'm counting on you, Dr. Stone." Then, per usual Miss Pearl fashion, she was gone in an eye blink.

She counted on me. Did that mean she considered me for the new position as well, or just Everett?

And was there even a position available?

I squared my shoulders and entered my own office.

If a job did exist . . . well, I would prove to her I was capable of doing that job and that she could count on me, even if that meant purposely throwing myself into the path of Everett Covington.

Chapter Eighteen

I started the very next day, showing up at Everett's office and knocking on his door. My heart thumped louder than the knock "Dr. Covington?" I said, peeking my head inside.

"Did you just call me Dr. Covington?" he asked from somewhere inside the room.

"Well, you *did* earn it," I answered.

"It's still weird to hear it out of your mouth."

"What are you doing?" I asked, entering the room a little more so I could see him.

He stood on the back of one of the chairs, balanced in a way that if he leaned in any direction, the chair would probably topple. His hands held a picture to the wall. I had to enter the room altogether to see the picture fully and could not contain the gasp of surprise when I saw what the heavy wood frame held.

The picture of us at a pretend tea making a toast over a stuffed bear. He'd had it enlarged into a poster sized and printed it up on canvas.

"What are you doing?" I asked again, only I felt certain the question seemed far more alarmed this time around.

"Claiming my office as mine," he said like it was no big deal.

"But that? That picture can't go up in this office, in this hospital . . . I have to work here too, you know!" Even though I lowered my voice, he had to know I was yelling at him.

But he completely, totally did not care.

He shrugged, making his chair wobble. I almost hoped he'd topple over after all and break some bones. Then I could hide the picture before anyone saw it. "What does it matter where you work? This picture is a work of art. It's my favorite picture. It goes where I go."

While I agreed that it had a look of actual art to it. I did not agree that it should go wherever he went. On that, I absolutely disagreed.

"Everett, this picture makes us look like we . . ." I sputtered for words and ended up sounding like an old car that wouldn't start.

He finally got the picture to snag on the hanger he must have inserted into the wall before I arrived. "Makes it look like we what?"

"Like we're . . . friendly."

"Are you saying we're not friends?" He stepped down from the back of the chair in a way that made the chair rock and tilt but not tip. So much for the broken bones option.

"Of course we're friends, but that picture looks like more than friends. It makes us look intimate, which is not professional at all."

He put his hands on my shoulders and drew me to him, which was also not professional at all. "Andrea without an E, this picture cannot come down until after the PR team has had its field day, done all of the interviews, and declared itself through with us. I'm sorry if it makes you feel uncomfortable, but Miss Pearl insisted."

His fingers were gentle on my shoulders. His eyes shifted color like they usually did but managed to stay brown longer than anything since they were emphasized by the brown of the shirt he wore under his lab coat.

"People will talk . . ." I tried again.

"Not any more than people talk about everything else. And when they're done talking, they will move on to something else. And this picture reminds me of one of the nicest days I'd ever had in my life and it will stay on my wall and make me feel some peace when I'm alone in my office—emphasis on the *my* part of that. You can put up pictures of waterfalls in your office, and I promise I won't complain."

He released me and moved behind his desk so he could survey his handiwork. "I'm awesome. It's not even crooked. But you aren't here to weigh in on my décor. What can I do for you, Andra?"

After another sputtering start, I managed to spit out, "I was just wondering how you were getting along here at the hospital and wondered if you needed any help with anything or if you needed any introductions."

Last night, I'd decided this was how I would approach Miss Pearl's assignment. Standing in his office underneath a picture that looked like a professional engagement photo, the idea of being seen in the halls with him filled me with dread. People would connect those dots fast, and how would that look?

Everett looked absurdly happy to have me suggest interaction and contact. I gritted my teeth and thought about Miss Pearl and her desire that the new doctor feel comfortable at Boston Children's. Miss Pearl would get what she wanted.

"I've seen pretty much everything, I think, but there are always things a guy misses. I have rounds to do this morning but can take a walking lunch before patients this afternoon? Sound okay?"

"Sounds great." I exited the office taking care not to look back in the direction of the picture.

Later, Becca helped me with a young girl who had come in complaining of chest pain that turned out to be a problem with her esophagus and not the angina her mother insisted the girl experienced. I took the few moments between the time the girl left and when the next patient would show up to tell Becca about the picture on Everett's wall.

"Hot doc has a picture of you on his wall? Can I start calling you pin-up girl?"

"Does everything have to go awkward with you? It's not that kind of picture! It's more a sweet, cozy . . ." as I sought for synonyms to describe the picture, I trailed off and thought about the fact that the picture did make me feel peaceful, just not when it was on Everett's wall! "Anyway, what the picture *is* isn't the problem. The problem is that the picture exists."

"Awwww, sweet and cozy? How is that a problem?"

I glared at her. "The difference between the sweet awwww and the horror stricken ahhhh is similar to the difference between the romantic poet and creepy, letter-writing stalker."

"So hot-doc is your stalker? And that's bad because . . .?"

"Because stalkers are generally considered bad, Becca."

"Are they?" She looked up from the vials of blood we'd taken to go down to the lab for testing "Even when they're hot? Because seriously, I would let that man stalk me any day."

"Who can stalk you?" Camille, one of the orderlies, asked.

"Don't you have someone to shave?" Becca crossed her arms over her chest. She was a little antagonistic to unruly orderlies, but in general, she liked Camille.

Her liking Camille meant that Camille didn't much care if Becca looked like she might get bossy. "Who's Dr. Stone's stalker?"

"The hot new doc," Becca supplied before I could shut her up. Did she really spill that information to a snoopy orderly?

"*Not* the new hot doc!" I insisted. "Not that I think he's hot or anything, but that I mean he is not stalking me."

Becca shot a look to Camille. "That isn't what she said a second ago."

I wanted to growl, face-palm, and stomp off to sulk somewhere, but leaving Camille in possession of such information was not an option.

"What I meant was, Dr. Covington is not stalking me. He's my friend. Only my friend. We've been . . . buddies for years. We did a photo shoot for his sister once, a long time ago. So I was just saying that people might think he's stalking me if they ever see the picture. But he isn't. Because we're friends. Just friends."

Becca and Camille shared the sort of facial expression one gets when one is very sick with stomach cramps or when one is in serious doubt. "That is definitely *not* what she said a minute ago," Becca said.

Where I had worried before about people thinking we were too friendly together if they saw us in the halls, now them seeing us friendly seemed imperative. Miss Pearl would not like me botching up her assignment to make him feel welcome by painting him as a creeper. Nothing could stop the rumor mill faster than me working hard to establish Everett and myself as the very best of friends.

So when I met Everett for our walking lunch, I smiled wide enough to force that smile to touch my eyes whether I felt actual happiness at seeing him or not.

But the thing was, when I saw him, I did feel actual happiness.

He came bearing Starbucks and Pockets Pizzas.

"These are bad for you, you know," I said.

"I absolutely know. My mother refused to buy them for me when I was a kid."

"My mom too." I took the proffered Pocket Pizza and, as had become our habit when consuming food or drink together, we tapped them to each other in a toast and bit in without any trace of guilt or shame.

Our mothers would have been scandalized.

The knowledge of that made the hot pocket taste that much better to me. "Pepperoni," I said. "Perfect."

"It's my favorite of the mystery meats. So where do you want to start your tour? I've got an hour."

I smiled. "Let's start at the beginning." I took him to the neonatal unit. Nothing had an earlier beginning than that. Though he had been taken to the unit by someone in Admin on his first day, he hadn't been introduced to everyone. I made sure to make introductions to my long-time friend from our pre-med days.

"How often do you end up with work in the NICU?" he asked me once all introductions were made and people went back to their work.

"Not terribly often. I've had a few cases that brought me this way, but none of these patients are mine currently." With the permission of the neonatologist, we peeked into an isolette at one of the sleeping infants. "It's a tough way to make a beginning in the world."

"But kind of awesome too," Everett said. "Twenty years ago, all the equipment here wouldn't exist. These babies wouldn't have the same chances. It's kind of awesome."

I agreed.

From there, we meandered through the halls splashed in kid-friendly colors and designs and visited several other departments where not all the staff had been there when he'd been introduced the first time. Most everyone already knew Everett, even without having met him. His reputation had gained a lot of popular traction. Everyone loved him—or at least liked him. And the few patients we visited along the way that belonged to him were thrilled he was their doctor.

In many ways, seeing the hospital through his eyes made me feel like he was the one giving me the tour. The new perspective made the entire place a little shinier. When our time was up, I dropped Everett back where I'd found him.

Before I could leave though, he said, "Hey! What time are you out of here tonight?"

"Kinda late," I answered.

"Me too. Want to go out and get a kinda late dinner together somewhere around here?"

He held my gaze for a moment while I debated and also while I wondered why I debated. "Sure," I said.

"Great. I'll meet up with you kinda later then." He laughed like he'd made a great joke.

When he was gone, I grudgingly laughed like he'd made a semi-decent joke.

"So. How are things going?"

I nearly jumped out of my skin. "Miss Pearl," I had to make a grab for my stethoscope before it clattered to the ground. "You scared me."

"So it would seem." Her dark hair was tied back into a ponytail and she wore scrubs with dragons that grinned mischievous smiles. Fitting even if it seemed a little out of the ordinary for admin to be in scrubs. That mischievous smile was echoed in Miss Pearl's own grin.

"Things are fine," I said. "It's nice to reconnect with Everett. He's a good friend from the past, you know." I wondered if she had seen the picture on his wall yet. She was bound to at some point.

"Yes. An interesting past the two of you share."

Camille hurried past on her way to somewhere, clearly in a rush,, but she had enough time to smirk at me on her way by. "It's not that interesting," I said, feeling a little insecure about her emphasis on the word interesting.

"You have an appointment right now, don't you?"

"Yes. I do, actually." My stomach flipped a little at her reminder. It wasn't like I'd forgotten or that I'd planned on getting to the appointment late. It was that she had stopped me and the idea of putting her off—even for a good reason—made my skin prickle.

"With the Henderson boy?"

"Yes," I said again.

"He's so tiny for his age."

He was tiny. In some ways that might have served his excessively weak heart well.

"I'll go with you," she said.

We turned in the direction of the clinic, with her content to chatter at my side. I'd almost tuned her out while thinking of Jamin Henderson and his inner fire and strength that did not make itself known physically, but came out loud and clear in personality and sheer gumption.

"I'm sorry, what did you say? A red string?"

"Yes. The red string of fate. You and Everett cross paths too often to be coincidence. In China, there was a legend or myth that said the gods sometimes, for purposes of their own, tied people together with their red string of fate. They tie your wrists or your ankles to the one you are destined to meet in your life, the one you are destined to be with in order to change the world for good."

Which was not what I'd been expecting her to say at all when she talked about us crossing paths. I held up my hands and turned them in various directions, trying to make a joke of her observations. "No string here."

"You can't see it, of course." She scoffed at me. "It's invisible."

I smiled and tried very hard to be patient with this strange sort of mystical nonsense. I didn't have time for magical voodoo. I was a doctor. Miss Pearl was *admin* for heaven's sake. Everyone knew admin never had any kind of imagination.

I tried to keep my face passive so Miss Pearl wouldn't know what I'd been thinking.

Sometimes I wondered why Miss Pearl took such an active interest in my life. She was likely one of my dad's friends, sent to spy on me, and my mom probably slipped her money every now and again to get Everett and I married off. My mother would love to have me marry a doctor. Becoming a doctor was not nearly good enough, not for my mother, not when she wanted me to have the time and freedom of a woman with a rich husband.

When I saw her last, I told her I could afford my own Versace. She said I purposely missed the point. But she was wrong. It wasn't on purpose. I simply just didn't get the point.

"You and Everett are unique." Miss Pearl brought me back to the conversation at hand.

Ah, yes, magical red string. "So who's stringing us along?" I asked, trying to be good-natured about the whole thing.

"The old lunar matchmaker god, who is in charge of marriages."

I couldn't help it. I laughed. "Did my mother send you?" I had to ask. The question was fair. Who else cared enough to worry about my dance card being full?

I stopped laughing when Miss Pearl scowled. "Your mother is simply benefiting from a lucky coincidence."

"What is this coincidence?" I asked.

"The two people connected by the red thread are destined lovers, regardless of place, time, or circumstances. This magical cord may stretch or tangle, but never break. Here in the West, they call this a soulmate or a destined flame."

Do not laugh, Andra Stone, I thought to myself.

"Do not laugh, Andra Stone," Miss Pearl said out loud, startling me a little that she seemed to know my thoughts. "You'll see. When fate brings you together again and again, it might just mean the universe is trying to tell you something."

"Or it might mean we're both working in the same narrow field, and meeting up is inevitable," I tried to reason.

"I like my theory better."

I smiled at Miss Pearl. How could anyone not smile? The ideas she spoke of were preposterous. Yet she seemed pretty dogged in her determination regarding them. "It's okay for you to like it, but you have to admit, your theory is a little . . . outdated."

She narrowed her eyes at me. "Love my house, love the crow on it. That's a Chinese proverb that says, you get exactly what you see." She nodded to the clinic door. "Get to work. And remember, I still expect you to take care of Dr. Covington."

"I won't forget what you expect."

How could I?

Hiding my grin proved more and more difficult the longer she kept talking. I'd never had a conversation on folklore with any of my peers before. The whole thing had been totally hilarious, even if it was a little disconcerting.

But as I worked throughout the rest of the day, I kept having the feeling that I had to give my hand an extra tug to make it do what I needed, as if it really was tied up with some red string or whatever.

At the end of the day, I stood in front of my window and tried to massage some feeling into my neck from bending over little people all day long. "This is what comes from not sleeping enough." I said out loud to my office.

"Don't tell me you thought this job would get you a regular

sleep schedule. You should have been a banker if you wanted that." Everett stood in my doorway, smiling at me and looking very much like the hot-new-doc rumor touted him to be.

I glanced at my wrist and frowned. *No red strings, Andra.*

"You okay?" he asked when I looked up and was apparently still frowning.

"I'm great. You ready to go?"

He nodded with gusto. His eyes sagged, and I felt a little guilty to be pulling him away from going home and getting sleep, but he'd invited me, not the other way around.

We walked in silence at first, but the silence didn't feel like the kind that had to be filled. Everett had always been like that for me, a space of relief, no pressure.

I frowned again.

Except for the time I mentally snapped after losing my scholarship. And then again when he stole my apartment. And then the last time when he had a girlfriend and didn't show up to my grandmother's funeral.

Those were lucky recollections because I felt too comfortable and too glad to be in his presence again, too much like fate had tried pulling a fast one on me.

"I think there's an opening for a surgeon." Everett said finally.

I experienced tachycardia because my heart rate had to be more than one hundred beats per minute. "I think you're right. Are you going to apply?"

He grinned a little sideways grin at me. "Will you still be my friend if I end up as your competition?"

"I'm not a total frosty tyrant yet. Of course you should apply. I don't know why I asked if you were. You would be an excellent addition." I was proud that I hadn't even missed a step while spewing any of those half-truths and sorta lies.

Because I felt a little like a frosty tyrant when it came to my career. I wanted the position a lot. The competitive side of me hated to lose at anything—especially not at the one thing I had worked my whole life for. But then I did also believe he should apply, and that he would be an excellent addition.

Was he my competition really? His newness to the hospital counted as a mark against him. "Don't worry, Andra," he said.

"Although I plan on applying, there is no way they'd ever favor me over you."

"I wouldn't be too sure about that. You have scary good skills with a scalpel."

"So do you."

We fell quiet again.

We didn't walk that far, just to Bertucci's Brick Oven restaurant. We'd frequented the one over at Faneuil Hall a lot back in the days when we were nothing but study buddies. I was glad of the nearness. It would keep us from being out too late so there was a chance of getting some sort-of sleep.

We entered the restaurant and got settled before Everett steepled his fingers and rested his chin on them. "Okay, you first."

"Me first what?"

His eyes glinted with more gold and seemed to match his playful mood. "How many hearts have you broken since we last were together?"

I actually laughed. That was definitely not the direction I imagined our first dinner conversation going. First? *Does that mean I anticipate more?* "Why do you think I'm going to tell you this information?"

"Because it's therapeutic. C'mon who else are you going to tell?"

"I have tons of friends I can tell," I said.

"Yes but none of your other friends will make you laugh and feel so good about breaking hearts while breaking up. C'mon. It's a fun game."

I threw my straw wrapper at him. "It's a weird game to play with your ex."

"That's what makes it more fun. Do you want me to go first?"

I considered this. I was kind of curious about his dating habits after me. I was desperately curious about Liz. If he wanted to be all open and weird about it, fine. I was in. "Sure. Go ahead."

He picked up the straw wrapper I'd thrown at him and rolled the white paper into itself. "Well . . . There's Liz who all but put an extermination order on me the day she showed up at my house to find you there."

"And who can blame her?"

He nodded. "Exactly. So she spent the next several months trying to convince me that I was wrong about her and me, and the only reason she actually gave up was because I moved. Okay. Now it's your turn."

"Uh-uh. It's still you. I already knew about Liz, so she doesn't count."

He'd been tightening the paper into itself. At those words, he flicked it at me. But he went again anyway.

By the time we were done with the "game" as he called it, I learned that he'd dated a gymnast named Michelle, who dislocated her shoulder while she was trying to show off to him by using a crumbly rock wall as a balance beam. He tried to get her to go to the doctor immediately since a fourth of all dislocated shoulders have a related fracture, but she only laughed it off and insisted she was fine because she was dating a doctor, which she insisted was close enough. The shoulder did turn out to be fractured, and he couldn't date her anymore after she'd blatantly ignored good sense. He'd also dated a lawyer named Lara, who got along too well with his sister Riley. There was an events manager who traveled all over the world and apparently kept boyfriends in several of her regular haunts; another doctor who involved herself in practices Everett considered unethical for a doctor, though he wouldn't tell me what those practices were; and an elementary school teacher who complained a lot about the unfair system that allowed doctors to make more money than teachers.

During that time, Everett learned that I dated a concert pianist named Michael, who told me that my musical talents were so low that I should just stick to playing the radio and making the choice not to sing along for the good of all society. Everett actually got mad about that guy and rushed to defend my vocal honor by saying he'd never heard anyone who sang as beautifully as me. The only time Everett heard me sing was when we were on the Charles River and we sang a duet from the play "Wicked" together, but I appreciated him sticking up for my vocal chords.

I told him about dating a professor named Terrance, who taught literature and refused to talk to me again when I told him I hated George Orwell's 1984. Even after I explained that I understood the importance the book has in society but that I just didn't like it for me personally, he continued on into a heated one-sided debate over all the many attributes that made the book the finest thing in literature since Shakespeare. Everett did not blame me for dumping that one, but he interrupted me when I mentioned my last semi-serious boyfriend.

Interrupted me and leaned in as though vastly interested. "You dated a busker? As in one who busks?"

"The very same."

He stared at me a long moment, took a bite of his pizza, then stared at me another long moment. "Did you have to pay for the dates?" he asked finally. "I mean, did he borrow money for rent?"

I shook my head. "He actually made really good money, better than the snobby professor."

"I always wondered about that. What did he do? What was his talent?" Everett hadn't been nearly so intrigued with any of the other guys and their stories, but the busker captivated him.

"Street magic. He was really good too. Sometimes I half-believed he really could make things disappear and reappear."

Everett scratched at his five o'clock shadow. "So he sounds pretty cool. What happened with him?"

I smirked. "Turns out I was better at disappearing than he was. One day I just knew it wasn't going anywhere and had to move on."

"Ouch. I just went from jealous of him to sorry for him."

"Leaving him was a kind truth," I said, recollecting a conversation we'd had so, so long ago.

We both fell silent after that, the game over. Surprisingly, talking about all those relationships had been pretty therapeutic and fun.

But with a few moments of time to consider the conversation, my mind wandered to dangerous places.

"Did you love any of them? Those other women?" I hated myself for asking the instant the words left my lips.

He leaned back in his chair and lifted his eyes from his empty plate to mine. "I've only ever been in love three times. None of those women made that list."

I wondered the identities of the other two when he clarified for me. "Three times. One woman."

The intensity of his gaze left no question as to the identity of that *one* woman.

"Oh," I whispered, unable to look away, unable to breathe, unable to think.

Was he saying he loved me still?

What would that mean to me if he did?

My heart felt like it was going into some sort of arrhythmia. How ironic would a heart attack be on a date like this? "Everett . . ."

"Do not say my name like that," he said.

"Like what?" I picked up my water glass and tried to hide my feelings in the act of taking a drink.

"Like you're considering a disappearing act."

I laughed, spraying water over him. I didn't even apologize for the spray. "You do know we work together. I'm not going anywhere."

"Good. I want us to be okay. Nothing weird between us."

"You mean aside from our convoluted dating history?"

"Yes. Aside from that."

"And from the fact that we're gunning for the same position at the hospital?"

"That's a minor inconvenience, but yes, aside from that as well."

I agreed with him. But we both knew that agreements and reality were not the same thing at all. In the interest of making the conversation less intense, I shifted the topic to Hazel and when she would arrive and what exactly was expected from me, and did Dr. Herald, the department chief, know about the little PR stunt?

I had to ask that last question because I had the feeling that Miss Pearl was the sort of woman who liked to do things under the radar if she could get away with it. Not that I blamed her. I liked things that way too. But this was one of those overly public times where under the radar was not going to work.

Dr. Herald was in favor of our PR stunt, according to Everett.

So admin approved. The physicians approved. There was nothing left to do but go through with the whole thing.

"When is Hazel coming?"

"It'll be a few months. Product development want to get the new toy right before they launch it to the hospital. And because it's going to little kids as well, they need to make sure it meets all the safety standards." He wiped his napkin over his mouth, an indication that dinner's end had come.

I stood and walked with him back to the parking garage. We discussed different places we lived, different reasons for leaving those places, and he finally told me what I hadn't been willing to listen to before.

"I didn't know you wanted that apartment," he said as we walked.

I rolled my eyes. "It so doesn't even matter anymore."

"You didn't talk to me again for *months* after that. Don't tell me it doesn't matter. But I had to get out of my apartment or I might have killed Adam."

"I had roommates to kill, too, you know."

"You probably did, but you would've wanted to add my roommate to your hit list if you had any idea what his plans for you were and if you had any idea the excruciating detail in which he explained those plans to me."

When I stared in disgust at Everett, he slid a sideways glance at me and shrugged. "I told you the guy was a player. You cannot believe how worried I was when you actually went out with him. I should've spray-painted *TOOL* on his car."

We stopped at the elevators and waited for the doors to slide open. I laughed. "Yeah, well . . . I can take care of myself."

"So you keep proving. I'm sorry about that whole apartment thing."

"I'm sorry about that whole leaving you at the Hatch Shell.

"You're forgiven," he said.

"Will you be so forgiving if I get the surgeon position?" I asked.

He hesitated before grinning wide and saying, "You would deserve that job."

He hadn't meant to hesitate, I was sure of that. He probably didn't even know he had hesitated, but I knew.

"What about you? Will you be so forgiving?"

Of course I said yes.

But I hesitated too.

Chapter Nineteen

Through the next month, Everett and I didn't date exactly—probably a direct result of our individual hesitations, but we gravitated toward one another in a way that felt unpreventable. We took lunch together more often than not. We sat by each other in staff meetings. We discussed ways to improve workflow and patient satisfaction.

We remained polite when the retirement of Dr. Mendenhall was officially announced. It would take a long time to choose and vet another physician. Everyone knew it. But everyone's eyes all went to where Everett and I sat next to each other. Those eyes all seemed to say, *let the games begin.*

We had officially become competition.

The thing about working at a hospital is that they move at a snail's pace to get anything done. It took them five months to hire Everett. It would likely take them at least that long, and maybe even longer, to decide on a surgeon.

If we'd been working for a private clinic, the decision would be made by physicians, and the process would be relatively short. At the hospital, everything was run by the people with the MBA's. They worked in a world of committee and paperwork.

Miss Pearl smiled a lot through the whole process. She acted cool and collected as she watched Everett and watched me and nodded as if satisfied with whatever it was she saw.

She smiled when Everett made puppets out of tongue depressors and entertained his patients and their parents, and half the staff. Of course, his antics made me feel like I needed children to leave my office laughing as well, so I made up jokes about tongues that were very sad when they left my office because tongue depressors did that sort of thing. Half the time the kids got the jokes and laughed, other times they blinked at me with big wide eyes.

Miss Pearl still smiled at me, even with my blunders.

Even as I felt the need to step up my game and prove I deserved the position, I also felt the pull of Everett's genuine friendship. If I had my hands full, he jumped to open the door for me. If I patted pockets, trying to find loose change for the vending machine, he was there to loan me a few quarters. If he caught me crying over patients in the hospital—even if they weren't my patients—he handed me a tissue without saying a word.

Likewise, If Everett failed to remember to take a lunch break, I handed him an apple or a protein bar from my stash of get-through-the-day-treats. If he felt frustration over symptoms of patients he couldn't place, I talked him through them until we had some plausible leads. If he snarked or growled at disorderly orderlies, I rolled my eyes at him and told him to stop being such a jack-wagon. He usually apologized to the orderly after that. It was usually Camille he had to apologize to.

We had a synchronicity to our friendship that worked like a precision timepiece. The mention of ex relationships with each other or with others was a source of friendly banter, instead of the awkward mess it could have been.

In all that, Everett didn't move to anything more than my friend. In all that, I resisted the urge to close my eyes and lean into him. Becoming competition shifted our friendship.

Competing with him was like staying in the same pose day in and day out, waiting for the photographer to finally snap the picture.

No one showed up at that stage in the medical career without a drive and ambition to see things through to the end. Everett was no different. Neither was I. We both wanted the job. We both wanted the position badly enough to not back off in order to give the other one space. His tenacity in spite of the fact that we had a tangle of unexpressed feelings toward each other made me respect him more, even if I didn't always like him.

Not liking him was part of that tangle of unexpressed feelings. Liking him too much was another part. Sometimes I tried to convince myself that I only looked after Everett's well-being because Miss Pearl told me to, and had yet to tell me to quit.

Had she given him the same directive?

Since she often took him aside and spoke to him quietly and his gaze inevitably slid toward me, I had to assume she'd told him to look after me the way I was supposed to look after him. Perhaps she did it to guarantee we would be able to work together regardless of who got the position. Perhaps she did it because she wanted the position to go to the one with the greater ability to show compassion under stress. Whatever her reason, it made me distrust the idea of Everett having feelings for me still. He loved the same woman three times. What were the chances of such an intelligent man being foolish enough to love that same woman a fourth?

Time passed quickly under the watchful eye of Miss Pearl and the eight surgeons who wanted to put in their own recommendations regarding us. And before I knew it, Hazel showed up with a whirlwind of activity. I had no appointments that day so that Hazel could boss me around as she saw fit.

And she did see fit.

She swanned in to the hospital amid camera flashes and an entourage, as though she walked the red carpet to a blockbuster premiere. Dr. Herald greeted her with wide smiles and hearty handshakes. They stopped for a few photos and then he brought her to me as if we'd never met before and needed an introduction.

She hugged me and said, "Let's get you set up for hair and makeup."

I cast Everett a bewildered glance as she took my hand and tugged me into my office. Her entourage wasted no time redecorating my office to look like a day spa. Mirrors, lighting, brushes and hair product, and a fold-up box of more cosmetics than could be found at any department store counter were all spread over my desk.

When a handful of hair pins that looked like torture devices tumbled out onto my desk, I shot a look in the mirror at Hazel standing behind me. "Does Everett have to endure hair and makeup?"

"Nope. This visit is about Doctor Andra Stone, the silent heartbeat of Boston Children's Cardiology."

"And that doesn't sound over the top to you?"

She bent down and put her face next to mine in the mirror. "The world will love it. I promise."

I totally called the hair pins. The stylist with the pink pixie cut working my head over stuck at least fifty of those pins straight into my scalp. No amount of scowling or *ow*-ing slowed the woman down.

By the time she was done with me, I had an up-do that no sensible doctor would ever want to endure, but it did look nice.

They did the interview first. And they did it in Everett's office so they had a good shot of the enormous canvas photo of Everett and me and the store launch. I was asked all kinds of questions regarding my position at Boston Children's; the type of interaction I had with the patients and why I decided to start being the hospital Santa Claus by sneaking in toys while the children slept.

Miss Pearl stood with Dr. Herald behind the cameraman. They both smiled at me with encouragement, so I decided to share the whole story.

"Well, there was this little girl named Zoe. She's a great kid. She loves unicorns and Thor, which I know is a funky combination, but those two things were her total favorites. She came in with end-stage heart disease. She was a candidate for a transplant. We used ventricular assist devices while she waited for a donor, but it had been a while. Some kids do really well on the VADs and can even go home and go to school while they wait for a donor. But the VADs didn't seem to be much help to Zoe. She worsened every day. The problem was that it wasn't just her heart that was failing her. She lost her will to fight somewhere in all the days of sitting on that hospital bed. Her will to live failed her every bit as much as her heart did.

"I just wanted to do something that might lift her spirits a little. So I found that she really liked reading. I went to a children's book store and bought her a bunch of books where the kids were heroes beating impossible odds. I hoped that if she could read about someone else fighting a huge battle and winning, maybe she would believe she could win too."

Someone behind the cameraman sniffed. I couldn't tell who the sniff came from, but someone else must have felt the same way I felt about little Zoe's situation. Telling the story made me want to cry as well.

"While I was at the bookstore, I saw a doll that held a book in her arms. The doll came from Hazel Covington's company, Second Childhood, and it hit me that I could not only help this one child, but I could help another child somewhere else in the world. I bought the doll and the books and left them in her room with a note that told her to pay attention to the heroes in the books."

"And what happened after that?" the interviewer asked.

I smiled and felt the tears burn hot at my eyes. I blinked them back since crying on interviews was incredibly lame. "She began to improve. She muscled her way through a lot of bad days until a donor came through. She's doing great now. I'm proud of her for realizing she wasn't powerless. Her heart might have been weakening, but that didn't in any way diminish her own power to be strong."

The interviewer flashed the camera a knowing smile. "This story, all by itself is filled with extraordinary generosity. But Doctor Stone didn't stop with this one child. No. She went on to provide toys and books to many other children in the hospital, even if they weren't being treated by cardiology. Doctor Stone has been the generous donor of over 150 toys for the residents of Boston Children's hospital. Tell us why you continued with the other children, Doctor Stone."

The hot lights set up for the cameras smothered me, and all the attention embarrassed me. But I answered the questions and explained my reasons for acting as I had. When the interview finished, they shooed me aside and interviewed a few of the other physicians, including Everett—who was asked to explain the significance of the portrait on his wall.

The whole thing made me blush vigorously and all felt kind of over the top until Dr. Herald gave me a wink and a thumbs-up before he walked away to attend to his own duties. But that thumbs up made all the circus worth it. That thumbs up was an approval from the department chief. Any approval would help me with consideration for the surgeon position.

During lunch, Hazel sat with me. Everett had appointments and everyone else faded away to their own meals.

"So you like working here?" Hazel asked.

"Love it. I can't imagine doing anything else with my life."

"Everett's the same way. This is all he's ever wanted to do. He turned out to be a pretty great kid, even if our Grace and Dad were a little whacked in actual parenting skills."

I smiled. Her parents were definitely different, but then, mine weren't much better, just an opposite side of extreme. I always imagined good parents landed somewhere in the middle. "He didn't turn out too badly, did he?"

"I was sorry with the way things ended between you two. I'm glad to see you're getting another chance."

I nearly coughed out the bite of spinach leaves I'd taken. A second chance? Did she not know that we'd already blown through a second chance and a third one as well? Did she not know how utterly not-going-to-happen Everett and I were as a couple?

I chewed with voracity and swallowed hard so I could clarify as quickly as possible. "We're just friends, now."

"Hm." She steepled her fingers and rested her chin on them, a female replica of her brother. "That's too bad," she said after a minute. "I mean, it's too bad that people think that the word *just* belongs in front of the word *friends*. Good friends make the best companions. I've always thought my parents' problems stemmed from the fact that they weren't ever really friends, you know?"

I gave a rueful smile. "My parents probably could have benefitted from a healthy dose of friendship, as well."

She shrugged and picked up her sandwich. "So maybe 'just friends' is something to think about?"

"We're also up for the same promotion."

She shrugged again and took a bite of her sandwich, the big kind of bite that let me know she had no intention of responding, which was too bad because I really wanted to know what she had to say about that. Hazel was a successful business woman. How would she handle a man she had a relationship with competing with her?

Her mother would probably hire a hit man to kill the competition off. My mother would bat her eyelashes, let him win, and hope she scored a ring out of the deal.

What would I do?

Second Childhood donated 500 toys to Boston Children's. Boston Children's signed a contract to carry Second Childhood toys in their gift shop and the whole day ended with a lot of congratulating and handshakes.

Hazel and Everett stayed with me while I cleaned up my office and prepared for the next day. "Any deliveries tonight, Santa Clause?" Hazel asked.

I grinned. "Sure. You guys can come along."

With the reporters and cameras gone, the brightly decorated halls felt blessedly silent. I took them to all my favorite places and peeked in on many of the sleeping children. Everett and I took turns giving brief medical histories of each child we looked in on so Hazel understood what was at stake for them.

I was surprised Everett knew so much about the kids—even the ones outside of cardiology.

Hazel frowned as we left the room of a little boy with leukemia. "What are the chances of him getting well?"

Everett was the one who answered. "It would be better if he believed in himself a little more—if he felt hope in his circumstances, instead of fear."

I felt a little frustration with his words. We provided comfort and reassurance as often as we provided real medical care. "I just wish that hope was something you could wrap up in shiny paper and tie off with a bow. I wish hope was as easy to give as a stuffed bear."

Everett jumped for a balloon string that belonged to a blue escapee balloon. He reeled it in and then tried to hand it off to me. When I refused to take it, he bit into the bottom of the latex and sucked in the helium. "Andra gives away hope all the time. She is the queen hope fairy! All hail, Queen Hope Fairy!"

Hazel and I both laughed at his high-pitched helium voice.

"Seriously, though," he said, his helium all spent and his voice normal again. "Wouldn't it be great if we could hand the kids a magic mirror that showed them a picture of themselves all grown up and doing the thing they want most to do with their lives and then we could tell them, 'See! This is who you get to be when you grow up. You have stuff to live for, so stop wallowing and start living!'"

I halted and put my hand on the wall to steady the sudden dizziness of excitement. "Everett! You're brilliant!"

Both he and Hazel also stopped. They stared at me.

"Don't you see? We *can* do that! Well . . . we can't, but Hazel can! What if Hazel made awesome heirloom hand mirrors, the kind that look like something out of Disney's Beauty and the Beast? And what if the face of the mirror is a canvas of some sort? We could hire an artist to come in and paint each child as a grown up doing what they want most to do with their lives? Any time they felt worried or nervous or whatever, they could just look in their magic mirror and see their futures."

Hazel picked up the excited vibe immediately. "That is a great idea! And it has a marketable potential too . . . granted, a little more generic and less personalized. Obviously we couldn't do hand-done original paintings, but we could do a digital sort of version that would be personalized enough to make parents want it!"

Everett had his one eyebrow raised. "Do you have any idea how much money it would cost to have hand painted originals on wooden mirrors?"

"Everett, stop being practical." Hazel hushed him with a wave of her hand. "We're brainstorming here. And we already said we'd do a digital version."

"Besides, Everest without an S. The Grandmother Foundation is financially secure for a while. I think we could do it."

Hazel grabbed my hand. "Want me to get started in research and development to see about costs and financial feasibility?"

"Yes!" I squeezed her hand and we started jumping and making hushed squeals in the hallway.

Everett clapped. "And this works out perfectly! Andra can go into business with you as a co-creator of toys, and I can take the surgeon job."

I stopped jumping, my stomach falling into my toes with the anger that took its place in my midsection. Hazel stopped jumping as well. She looked like she might throw a punch at him for messing up the moment.

I turned and smiled sweetly. "Aw, Everett . . . screw you very much for that vote of confidence. I am absolutely *not* backing out of the surgeon position, so don't you dare go getting comfortable. I fully plan on being a surgeon in this hospital."

I turned and gave Hazel a hug. "Thanks for the nice day." I walked off down the hall the opposite way without saying goodbye to Everett.

I heard a loud "Ow! Hazel!" from Everett so I figured she must have let that punch fly. I didn't care. How dare he say that to me? How dare he minimize me in that way so he could scoot me conveniently to the side and take the job I'd worked my whole life for?

I hoped Hazel left a bruise on him.

And I had the answer to my earlier question. Everett's mother was the sort of woman to hire the hit man and remove her competition once and for all. My mom was the sort of woman to flirt her way into marriage by giving up the competition. And me?

I was the sort of woman who fought to win.

Chapter Twenty

He tried to apologize, following me around all the next day with phrases like, "I was only kidding around" and "You know I think you've got a better chance than I do; I was just blowing off steam" and "Haven't you ever said something stupid you wish you hadn't said before?"

To the last question, I said, "Yes," and shut my office door in his face. I frowned once inside the privacy of my office. The truth was that I had a pretty good chance at the job, probably better than he did, and a lot of that chance stemmed from the fact that Everett had called his sister and given me a day to show off for admin.

The race had been pretty neck and neck until yesterday, but now I swelled with a confidence I didn't really deserve because I hadn't really earned it. Everett had earned it for me.

That fact really bothered me.

Because I was mad at Everett. Because I didn't like him very much at the moment. Because I actually did care about him even while not liking him. Because he had really hurt my feelings.

Again.

"How many times am I going to have to forgive this guy for being a mess?" I asked myself while washing my hands in the ladies room.

"As many times as he is a mess."

I jumped and ended up splashing water all over the mirror. "Miss Pearl! You scared me!"

"So the mirror would indicate. Having trouble with Dr. Covington?"

"No," I lied and pulled paper towels from the dispenser to wipe the mirror down.

"Go easy on the boy. It's a hard thing for him too." She watched me scrub streaks into the mirrors. "I've heard it said you should love someone when they least deserve it, because that's when they need your love the most."

"Chinese proverb?"

"No. Swedish."

The unexpected comment made me laugh outright. For being in an uptight admin position, Miss Pearl was okay. Complaining about the guy she could very well choose over me would be like kissing a viper and expecting not to get bitten. Complaining to anyone in management always made the complainer look bad and never solved anything. So I dropped the subject of Everett entirely.

"You did very well yesterday with the TV and cameras and interviews. And your ideas to make the lives of these children emotionally better are good ideas. I'm glad you've worked so hard to be a doctor. This hospital is so obviously a place where you belong. But don't belong so well that you give up the other place where you belong even more."

Some other women entered the bathroom and Miss Pearl slipped out while I greeted them. I scowled at my streaked reflection in the mirror. I understood why she wanted her doctors to get along. Grumbling physicians made a bad environment for everyone, including their patients.

But understanding why she wanted us to get along and wanting to actually get along were not the same thing.

Everett and I became cool acquaintances after I refused to accept his apology. He apparently didn't like getting a door slammed in his face, but I didn't like him acting like a tool with me, so we were even. The fact remains that he wouldn't have said he wanted me out of the way so he could be promoted if he hadn't been really thinking it.

And sure, I wanted the position too, but at least I had the decency to feel conflicted about it. At least, I had felt conflicted. From the point I shut the door in his face, all the conflict disappeared. He was my competition only. And he was toast.

Whereas we'd previously sat together at staff meetings, we now chose places opposite each other. Whereas we'd often eaten lunch together before, I'd taken to picking my food up and eating it in my office while I studied up on problems my patients dealt with so I could better help them. Whereas, we before had joked and bantered, we were now civil to the point of frostbite.

If one of the surgeons praised Everett for working such long hours, I stayed even longer the next day, even if I had nothing to actually do. If they mentioned he was patient with the nurses,

I smiled until my cheeks hurt and until Becca finally told me I looked like a creeper. If his patients left smiling, mine left with the entire sucker bowl and the whole roll of Disney stickers. If Everett was doing it, I was right there working to do it better.

Everett's actions were mirrors of my own. Praise showered on me for any little thing would be the thing Everett worked on next. Anytime the surgeons said anything, Everett and I dashed to outmaneuver the other.

Someone—probably Miss Pearl—put us on opposing schedules to relieve some of the tension in the building. Everett ended up working more nights and I ended up working more weekends.

Admin couldn't be blamed for the schedule shifts, but the new adjustments made it more time consuming to keep up with Everett because then I had to sleuth around to find out all the great things he did, so I could do them better.

The whole process had grown quite tedious.

Becca didn't even bother to hide her amusement over the whole thing. After returning from one such circus event where I was helping with some new medical students who sang praises to Everett's name any time he was mentioned, she shook her blonde curly head at me. "You are some kind of pathetic, you know that?"

"I am horribly aware of that fact, yes." I sat in her chair and rested my forehead on her desk. "I don't know how much longer I can keep this kind of pace up."

"Hmph. While I love how efficiently everything runs with the two of you one-upping each other, I'm not really interested in watching you break, honey. Why not call it a truce?"

"With Everett? No. Never. Not happening. You know our history."

"History schmistory. You told me he was your best kiss."

"He also was involved in me losing my scholarship."

"You know that was your fault."

I stared at the ground with the swirly patterns in the carpeted area under her desk and considered the whole situation. "Actually, no. It's his fault. He was the one who got the paint can from my friend who was trying to keep me from painting Greg's truck. If he hadn't done that, I would have gone home and forgotten the whole thing."

I heard her blow a raspberry. "But who bought the paint can?" Curse her logic.

"Well," I said, knowing I had ammunition to play the everything-is-Everett's-fault game all day. "He stole the apartment I'd been waiting for over a year to move into. That was totally him."

"Did he know you wanted it?" She tugged at a paper that was on her desk and also under my head so that it jerked out from under my forehead. "You're getting my paperwork oily from your moisturizer." Her voice had a scowl to it.

"Sorry." I thought about my situation with Everett and tried one last time to prove to Becca that he was my nemesis. "He never called after my grandma died."

She hesitated before she said, "Okay, I'll give you that one. But only that one. I just don't like seeing you like this. You were happier when you liked him. You guys went from good friends to claws and teeth and all for what? A job?"

"It's not just a job. It's *the* job. The thing I've worked for from the beginning, and he's trying to take it away from me!"

Becca smirked. "You do realize that the whole world is not all about you, right? This job is also the thing *he's* worked for from the beginning. Only for him, *you're* the one stealing the prize."

I tilted my head so I could look at her without lifting my forehead from her desk. "Careful. Or I won't like you anymore either."

She laughed. "I'm just saying a little perspective might help you here with Hot-Doc."

That was Everett's nickname throughout most of the female staff. I tried not to be irritated by the blatant sighing that followed him through the halls.

"I just think you should let this whole dispute go. You're too competitive for your own good. I get ambition, I really do, but you and Hot-Doc are taking it all to an unhealthy level."

"Are we talking about Hot-Doc?"

I lifted my head to see the newcomer. Camille blinked in surprise at me. "Oh . . . hi, Dr. Stone. I didn't know you were back there."

She shot a look of alarm to Becca, who rolled her eyes. "You're not in trouble, Camille. Dr. Stone knows everyone calls him that."

Camille looked suspicious. "And you're okay with that?"

I shrugged. "Why would I care?"

Camille shrugged as well, her tiny shoulders shifting under the thin cloth of her scrubs. "I thought you two were . . ."

With serious effort, I did not growl at the girl. "We're not."

She brightened considerably. "Oh! Then maybe you won't mind if I ask him to go clubbing with me. I hadn't asked because I really thought you two were . . . but you're not. That's awesome."

She scampered away looking altogether too pleased with life.

I leaned back in Becca's chair and glared at Camille's retreating back. "If he accepts her offer, it will prove he is beyond stupid and will justify me killing him in his sleep."

Becca smirked at me and tucked her pen in her hair behind her ear. "You wouldn't say that if you didn't like him."

"Yes, I would. Because I don't like him, and I did say it, so clearly you're wrong. I guess I should just be glad it wasn't Miss Pearl catching me diss on Everett. She would not like that one bit."

"Where has that woman been lately anyway?" Becca asked, looking around as if Miss Pearl would pop up out from under her desk, which, with Miss Pearl, the possibility existed.

"She said she had other people to take care of since business here was taking so much longer than she'd expected."

"No thanks to you and your cold war with Hot-Doc."

I shoved out of the chair. "I'm going to go check in on Max. Someone said he's not doing so well."

"Or you're checking on him because you're trying to escape hearing the truth from me."

I didn't respond, so Becca smirked at me as I rounded the desk to the front counter, and as I rolled my eyes at her, and probably as I walked away.

I really despised that girl's smirk.

Visiting Max turned out to be my best idea of the day. His dark hair stuck out in all directions from his head since he was stuck in a hospital bed, but the mussy hair managed to make him look cute instead of orphaned like it did some of the kids staying with us.

"I hear you're having a birthday soon," I said to him when he looked up from the Lego set spread out over the sheets in front of him.

His demeanor shifted from focused to excited. "I do! I'll be eight! In just six days!"

"Eight is so old." I pulled up his chart on my iPad. "I'm going to have to buy you a cane and a set of false teeth."

"Better get you some old lady diapers while you're at it, cause I'm not as old as you!" he shot back with a grin so wide that it revealed the gap of his last missing tooth in the back.

I laughed. "But you will be. Someday, you will be as old as me and you'll need diapers, too."

"If I live forever and you live forever, then I will never be as old as you because you were born first." The kid was born with a quick tongue and a sharp wit. He was seriously the highlight of my day every day. He was on the donor list. The VADs had worked for him for a while so he could stay home and live his life like normal, but they'd become less effective as time went on, and now he was back in the hospital.

Max wasn't my patient, but we interacted enough to know we were good buddies. He was among the first kids who got a Second Childhood toy. When he'd been readmitted to the hospital, I was gratified to see he'd brought his big stuffed dinosaur with him, and it never left his side.

Max was Dr. Mendenhall's patient. But Dr. Mendenhall included both Everett and me in the details of the boy's progress, keeping us trained on the tough cases—the ones that were rare and much more complicated.

"What are your plans for your big birthday?"

"I'm gonna have a party here in my room. My mom's bringing my friends over and we'll have cake and ice cream and stuff."

I nodded and tried not to frown at his information on my screen. "Sounds great, buddy, but only if I'm invited."

He scrunched his face up in what I was sure he meant to look like extreme skepticism. "Are you cool enough to come to my party?"

I sat on his bed, picked up some Legos, and built a little tower of blue and red. "I dunno. Are you cool enough to invite me?"

"I guess you're invited, but don't go wearing any lame party hats. I already told my mom, no lame party hats." He nodded emphatically as if to convince me.

Which meant I was totally going to wear a lame party hat. I'd have to go to a party store to find the lamest one available. I'd get one for Max as well. Maybe I'd get him a feather boa too—just for laughs. I stuck the tower I'd made on top of what look like a landing pad for the space ships he'd been building. "Control tower," I explained as I stood.

He didn't remove the tower, which had to mean he didn't think the addition to his creation to be completely unworthy.

"Do you need anything?" I asked him, looking around the room and his shelf filled with books and games and his walls with posters featuring characters from an X Box game I wasn't familiar with. "I can sneak you some extra Jell-O or pudding or some green beans since I know they're your favorite."

"I'll get you some shrimp on a stick since that's *your* favorite," he shot back.

"Mmm . . . shrimp on a stick. Dip it in habanero sauce and get me a barf bag."

Max laughed that little boy giggle that filled the room. Best Sound. Ever.

I mussed up his already-mussed up hair which made him scowl and swat me away.

"So I saw that interview of you on TV," he said as I was leaving.

"What interview?"

"The one about the toy store. It was on YouTube. You gave me the dinosaur . . . didn't you?"

I made a pshaw noise and shook my head. "Me? Give you something? That would mean I would have to like you."

"You *do* like me," he insisted with a smugness that would either get him slapped or adored by teen girls everywhere when he got into high school. "Everybody likes me because I'm awesome."

"You *are* awesome, Max."

"Thanks Andy. For the dinosaur." He'd started calling me Andy when he heard my brother's nickname for me when Nathan came in once to visit.

"You're welcome, buddy. Get to sleep before Nurse Randall comes in and slaps some obedience into you."

He snickered at the mention of Nurse Randall because he felt guys shouldn't be nurses. I told him he'd change his mind when he finally achieved a liberal arts education—which is where he always tuned me out because he had no idea what I was talking about.

I went home feeling pretty good—even if Becca had defended Everett, and even if Camille actually had the nerve to ask if she could date Everett.

When I returned to the hospital for my next shift, I was met at my door by the very same guy who had been the bane of my existence since I'd met him.

I was about to ask him what he thought he was doing in my space when my question cut off with just one word.

"What?" I asked as soon as I laid eyes on his wrinkled clothing, disheveled hair, and sunken eyes.

His eyes were green and gold and shiny with what I believed to be tears. "Max was taken in to surgery last night."

Chapter Twenty-One

Max.

My Max.

The kid who made barf jokes and who could pass gas on command. The kid who thought I was hilarious and who let my control tower stay on his Lego board. The little boy who was supposed to be turning eight in just five days!

I froze at Everett's words, liquid ice in my veins shooting through my entire body. "What happened?"

"I don't know what triggered it. But Max became unresponsive with agonal respirations and a wide complex tachycardia consistent with ventricular tachycardia. We were able to resuscitate him and Dr. Mendenhall took him in immediately. I assisted in the surgery. He's stable. They're watching him. I just thought you would want to know, so I stayed to tell you." He edged past me, obviously intending to leave.

"Everett . . ."

He turned, but only slightly. The slump of his body dragged on him. How was he even still standing?

"He's going to be okay?"

Everett nodded as though his head were filled with sand. "He's stable, Andra. He needs a donor. But for now . . . he's okay."

"Everett . . ." I didn't know what to say to him, only that him leaving felt so wrong and saying his name out loud gave me a comfort I couldn't explain.

When he turned to look at me again, I went to him, wrapped my arms around him, kissed his cheek, and whispered, "Thank you. For helping him. For telling me. For staying. Thank you." I released him, and he nodded and finally left.

During my rounds, I checked in Max's room. The dinosaur stood watch from atop the pillows of the freshly made bed. The dinosaur seemed to be waiting for Max to return from post-op. It looked forlorn and wrong there without the boy.

I frowned and returned to my own work.

He's going to turn eight, I thought to myself. *And then nine and ten and twenty-five.*

Wasn't that why we did what we did? So they would keep growing?

By the time I returned home that evening, it occurred to me that I hadn't once thought of outdoing Everett. Everett had helped save Max's life. How could anyone outdo that? Being a surgeon wasn't a game. It wasn't some contest. It was about hiring the right person to do the job. From the rumors running among the staff throughout the day, Everett had been efficient, proficient, quick, and steady. Dr. Mendenhall had applauded him.

Everett was the doctor of the hour.

He'd been the right person for the job.

And I didn't even envy the rank.

I was only grateful.

Which was why, several days later, when Max was back in his room looking only slightly worse for the wear, I decided to throw the best birthday party any eight year old with a failing ticker deserved.

And why I invited Everett to go shopping with me to get all the cool party fixings available.

To my surprise, Everett offered to drive. To my greater surprise, he showed up exactly when he told me he would. I had actually anticipated him cancelling on me via text at the last minute.

Unfortunately, I wasn't smart enough to keep that thought to myself.

"Why would I cancel?" he asked, clearly already frustrated, and I hadn't even opened the door to the front seat yet.

I grunted. "That comment isn't a reflection of your character." I did open the door then, and actually sat down on the passenger side of the car, swung my legs in and buckled myself into the seat so he couldn't change his mind about going with me without forcibly removing me from his car. "It's a reflection of mine. I've been a little cold lately, and you haven't totally deserved it."

"A little cold? The frost giants from Nordic legend are like a cozy campfire compared to the way you've treated me."

"You started it," I reminded him.

"And I said I was sorry."

"Yes, but by then, I had decided we were at war and I needed to crush my opponent."

"So what? You concede the war, now?"

"No!" I shot him a look. Was he really suggesting I give up again? "I'm still very much going for the position. I just want to be friendly about it."

He stood there, with his hand on his open car door, and his eyes fixed on me. I wondered for a moment if he planned on forcibly removing me after all, but instead he nodded. "Good." He shut the car door and moved around to the driver's side.

He got in, his jaw muscles flexing as if he were biting back all the things he wanted to say and chewing them very carefully. He set his GPS to find the closest party supply store near us and began driving.

"I accept, by the way . . . your apology, I mean."

"Thank you." He turned onto Storrow Drive.

"And I apologize as well."

"Apology accepted." He didn't even ask what I was sorry for. I might have asked if it had been me. And then he looked at me with a smile so completely satisfied that I almost wanted to slap him.

"You actually apologized!" he blurted out as if I'd done something unheard of.

"Wipe that smug off your mug, or it will never happen again."

He tried to look contrite, but failed miserably as he pulled into the parking lot of the party supply store his GPS led us to.

Being mad at Everett for feeling surprise at my apology would be like being mad at someone feeling surprise that the sun failed to give off light during an eclipse. Surprise was a healthy response to the rarity of the event.

With the apologies given and accepted, everything felt mostly normal. We bought ridiculous party hats, the kind that blinked in the most obnoxious way possible. We also bought matching blinking birthday badges and a feather boa that Everett promised to wear. When we finished with our purchases, we drove back to my house in relative silence until Everett cleared his throat.

"I'm sorry that this position got in the way of us getting along. And I'm sorry I want it so much that I allowed that to happen."

"We both want it so much. We've worked our whole lives for this one objective. It was bound to get crazy."

"Definitely crazy. We were a little out of control there for a while. I think I had an anxiety attack any time Dr. Herald mentioned how astute you were or how nice you were. I swear if I heard one more thing about your impeccable bedside manner, I might have tossed a bed on its side and screamed 'how's that for bedside manner?'"

I laughed. "I know what you mean. Dr. Mendenhall loves having you assist because 'Nobody stitches a cleaner line than Dr. Covington.'" I gave my best imitation of Dr. Mendenhall's gruff voice.

He laughed with me. "That's what Doctor Niles said about me too. He even put it in the recommendation for residency. The day I was accepted to Johns Hopkins for residency was the first and only time my mother ever told me she was proud of me. I think that's part of why I want the surgeon position so much. I want to prove to her that I succeeded. And what's crazy is she probably still won't approve."

His need for that approval felt achingly familiar.

"I'm sorry if I've been frost giant frozen over this," I said. "I've never been the sort of girl to back down from a contest and it's been hard to see this any other way. It's my worst trait. Grams used to call me a mountain of pride that was ready to avalanche on the first person who dared to challenge me."

He grinned, "She really did know you, didn't she?"

"She really did." I stared at my window, thinking about her, about the position, about who I'd become when she hadn't been around to see. "I called her, you know . . . the day they approved my surgical residency at Boston Children's. The line rang twice before the phone chimed in my ear and that overly-friendly digital woman's voice informed me that *the number you have called has been disconnected.* I was so excited, I forgot she wasn't there anymore. Hearing that voice was like losing her all over again. I just forgot." My vision blurred with the memory.

"I'm sorry, Andra."

"I know. Sometimes hard things change people for the better. After losing Grams, my dad relaxed a lot. He became pretty supportive of me and my medical career and of Nathan and his cooking career. So out of ashes, comes a rebuilding, a strengthening. Or so they say anyway."

We both fell silent. We were almost to my house. What was there left to say? We had dreams and ambitions and hurts and . . . it was all so overwhelming.

"I thought you were mad at me," he said once he turned down my road.

"What?"

"You left during that whole mess with Liz and I tried to call you, but you never answered and never returned my calls. I thought you were mad. So I figured I would let you have some space and try to work it out later. I didn't know about your grandma. Not until much later and by then, I felt pretty stupid and horrible and didn't know how to approach you again. You were so broken during that time. I don't think you even saw me when we were in the same room together. I don't think you saw anything."

I stretched my mind back to those days, those moments. Had he called? My only memories were of blind panic on the train after getting my brother's text. He might have called. I might have ignored such a thing.

"I don't think I saw anything either," I said. The car stopped at the curb in front of my house. I turned to Everett. "It's okay, Everett."

Miss Pearl spoke of a red string that bound certain people together. If any such string existed, it would have snapped under all the pressure of tugging and pulling between Everett and me.

I exited the car with a new sort of respect and understanding. We both had our reasons for doing what we did. Right or wrong. The reasons existed. And we each felt validated in our own point of view.

Not that I had any intention of telling Becca I'd figured out how to see things from Everett's point of view. The gloating would never stop if she found out.

We threw the best and biggest party for Max that the hospital had ever seen. Max laughed a lot. His mom and dad held each other a lot and hovered close to their son, a hand on his shoulder or on his leg, in some way staying connected to him as if they were afraid to let go. I thought again of Miss Pearl's string and could finally see what she might have meant. Some people were totally connected—tied together, sharing each other's fates.

Everett and I sang several songs in key helium for the group of children gathered in Max's room. The kids laughed. Max wore his obnoxious party hat with pride.

I watched Everett with the children, watched the way he talked to them without talking down to them, the way he listened when they spoke as if every word about the latest video game was actually important, the way he wasn't afraid to get silly and smear cake on his nose and pretend he didn't know what everyone was talking about when they told him he had something on his face. Everything he did was just for the smile it would bring to those watching.

Everett made the party a complete hit.

A donor came through for Max the very next week. He would live to be nine and ten and twenty-five.

Max would live.

Everett was asked to assist in the surgery.

Chapter Twenty-Two

Miss Pearl returned a few weeks later. With her return was the rumor that the board had decided on a new surgeon.

Watching Max strengthen had strengthened me as well. The clear choice was Everett. Even *I* would have chosen Everett over myself. And that was the clincher for me.

I chose him.

Something had happened during the situation with Max. I opened my eyes and really saw Everett and all the ways he was and all the ways he could be. Something Miss Pearl said came back to me: *You can fall in love and live a lifetime in one single moment.*

Watching Everett with Max was a single moment. The epiphany came without any fanfare or excitement. It crept in quietly, nestled down inside my heart, and declared itself at home.

So when the day came that we were to finally discover who would receive the position, I dressed nicely and went to work fully prepared to shake the victor's hand.

Miss Pearl met with me first.

She apologized for the amount of time it took for the hospital to make a decision. And then she apologized that I had not been selected but that it was in no way a reflection on my grand ability or work ethic. The decision had been made with many considerations and blah blah blah. I stopped listening since not getting the position didn't affect my confidence the way I thought it might.

I was a good physician. I would continue to be a good physician.

Plus, I had a toy in development that I helped create.

Not expecting to be awarded the position made the sting of the reality very quick and painless, like when we told children shots would only be a little pinch and then everything would be fine.

It really was a little pinch. Everything really was fine.

I exited Miss Pearl's office and saw Everett standing there, waiting his turn. I couldn't help myself. I grinned wide and gave him a thumb's up. He smiled back and returned the gesture.

I waited for him because there were things to say, and I had no idea if I would have the strength to say those things later.

Everett exited Miss Pearl's office with a look that could only be described as relieved. At that moment, I knew he got it: the job we'd both worked so hard to get, the job we'd nearly ruined ourselves over.

And I couldn't be unhappy.

I smiled at him, feeling my own relief in that moment. No more strings tied us to some unspoken feud. The only string around us now was the one Miss Pearl had told me about, the red string of fate. Our string was a string of friendship, tested, tried, and found to be true. Everett was my friend, and at that moment staring across the room at him, all I wanted was his happiness.

He smiled back at me and we crossed the room. After all, it was right to shake the winner's hand. When we met in the middle, we skipped the handshake and went straight for the hug.

"Congratulations!"

We pulled back and shared a startled look of incomprehension.

We had *both* said congratulations.

"You got the job, didn't you?" Everett said over my, "The job is yours, right?"

We shared another startled look.

"Wait," I said.

"Hang on a second," he said.

"Didn't you?" I said.

"I was sure that you . . ." he said.

"But I didn't," I confirmed.

"I didn't either," he offered as if to explain.

But explain what? What had just happened?

We burst into laughter, shared another hug and another round of congratulations.

When we broke apart, I wiped at tears in my eyes from laughing so hard. "Well this was certainly not what I expected from today."

"Nothing at all what I'd expected either. I'd come into the office prepared to give the position up to you. You deserve it. You've worked so hard. The kids love you. You make this entire place better."

Gratitude for his faith in me filled me and spilled over. "And what about you. How many times have you made the right call in the critical moment and a life was saved? Everett, you're a hero within these walls. I'm actually thinking about buying you a cape."

"Well, how about that. Andra Stone thinks well of me." The playful words hid the bite of hurt that existed between us after all these years of ebb and flow, of chances blown away like dandelion seed. He actually moved away a step, turning to leave. "That's something, isn't it? It might even be enough to get me through after I'm gone."

"Gone?" My throat constricted with alarm.

"I've been offered another job, Andra. I couldn't, you know I can't continue like this . . . It's best we both—"

I had to do it. I had to say the words I had never been brave enough to say before. The chance my feet stood in was the last one. I felt it to the core of my being, the knowledge shaking my bones inside my skin, the surety pounding through me with every beat of my heart.

"It's more than that, Everett," I interrupted him before he said something we wouldn't be able to recover from. "It's more than me thinking well of you. I came in today to congratulate you as well. I had every intention of walking away from this position, knowing you deserved it, knowing you deserve every happiness, and knowing I've screwed up so much of your life, but also knowing I have to tell you the truth."

He closed his eyes and sucked in a hard breath. "I don't know that I'm up to any more kind truths." He scratched at the back of his head and backed away another step. I grabbed his hand, like he had grabbed mine three times before.

As soon as our fingers touched I felt something soft loop over our wrists, but when I looked, nothing was there but our hands. I rushed on before he could try to pull away. "I don't know if it's a kind truth. I don't know if it's kind to either of us, but it has to be said, while there's still time to say it."

I swallowed the lump in my throat that had moved into the

way of my confession, making me stumble and stutter and need to start again.

"I . . . Everett, I . . ." Our eyes locked, his eyes more green than brown or gold. "I love you."

The words hung in the air like the last bit of light from a brilliant, chandelier-style firework just before it died in the darkness. In that moment of suspension, I felt fear like I'd never felt before.

I was too late. *Oh, Miss Pearl . . . I wish I had listened to you sooner. I am too late.*

"Well then . . . That makes this interesting, doesn't it?" he said.

I swallowed hard.

"It's only fair to tell you that I, uh, I love you, too."

"What? Even after—"

"Yes. Even after." His fingers tightened on mine. "And there are a lot of even-afters in our relationship. For both of us."

He leaned in and I moved to close that distance, to close it once and for all and never let anything come between us again.

But the office door opened and Miss Pearl stepped out, her arms folded across her chest. She leaned into the doorframe and waited. When we stood still, wondering what to do with her interruption, she said, "Well? Go on! I think I've actually waited longer than the two of you for this moment, and I won't be denied yet again."

"Did she just tell us to—"

I cut him off with a kiss. We had *all* waited too long. And I was done waiting. When I broke away to breathe, I glanced back to see if Miss Pearl still watched.

She was gone.

I expected her to be gone and was surprised by the disappearance at the same time. Everett seemed to have forgotten she was ever there.

"Would you like to go to dinner?" he asked. "Every night for the rest of our lives?"

"I think that sounds kind of perfect."

"You still smell like a lemonade stand." He stood so close that his lip brushed mine when he spoke.

"You still smell like cinnamon," I whispered.

He still had a hold of my hand and with the other, he cradled my face, his fingers threading into my hair behind my ear. His mouth settled softly on mine.

As we tangled into each other, the fingers from our free hands twined together, that soft sensation of something looping over our hands returned.

Only this time, the loop was pulled tight, binding us to that moment, to that tangle, to our two hearts, and the universe snicked into place and stayed put this time.

After all, when you meet the same guy over and over again, it just might mean the universe is trying to tell you something.

The End

Dear Reader,

Thank you for reading *Four Chambers*! *The Power of the Matchmaker* series has been in the works since 2014, and I hope you'll enjoy all the other books in the Series. They all have the linking character, Miss Pearl, but they can be read in any order. If you haven't read Pearl's story yet, check out *Power of the Matchmaker*, the novella.

If you'd like to join my Review Team and receive e-book copies in advance, please send me an e-mail at jules@juliewright.com.

Reader reviews help me spread the word about this book. So, if you have the time, please post a review on Amazon or on Goodreads.

Thanks for your support!

Acknowledgments:

I am lucky enough to be surrounded by amazing people who invite me to be part of their amazing plans, and no amount of thank-you will ever be enough, but thank you Heather Moore! This book would not exist without you. It's a story I've wanted to write and had been in my idea file for over a decade, but I likely never would have sat to write it all out without you! I'm grateful for all the talented authors who are a part of this series with me: Heather Moore, Rachael Anderson, Karey White, Kelly Oram, Heidi Ashworth, Taylor Dean, Michele Paige Holmes, Janette Rallison, Regina Sirois, Sheralyn Pratt, and Jaima Fixsen. Thanks to my support writers who make this journey as a writer so worth being on: you all know who you are. A special thanks to Rachael Anderson for her cover design. She's crazy good at what she does and understands the romance market. Thank you to Crystal Liechty for her editing prowess and for allowing me to name characters after her in various forms throughout the book, but mostly for her friendship. And, finally, thank you to my husband and children for your patience while I write, your support, your endurance, and your love. You people are my world. And always, thank you to my readers. What I do is nothing without you.

12 Novels by 12 bestselling authors in 12 months

Power
of the
Matchmaker
— SERIES —

November 2015...Power of the Matchmaker
(A prequel novella of the Matchmaker's story)

January 1, 2016

February 1, 2016

March 1, 2016

April 1, 2016

May 1, 2016

June 1, 2016

July 1, 2016

August 1, 2016

September 1, 2016

October 1, 2016

November 1, 2016

December 1, 2016

www.ingramcontent.com/pod-product-compliance
Lightning Source LLC
Chambersburg PA
CBHW070700280626
47159CB00022B/1671

* 9 7 8 1 9 4 1 8 4 9 0 6 4 *